Stirrings

STIRRINGS

Maryann D'Agincourt

PP

Portmay Press

New York

 This is a work of fiction. Names, characters, businesses, places, events, and incidents are either the products of the author's imagination or used in a fictitious manner. Any resemblance to actual persons, living or dead, or actual events is purely coincidental.

Cover image: *New York City, Bird's Eye View*, 1920, Joaquín Torres-García

Printed in the United States of America

ISBN 978-1-959986-31-7 (paperback)
ISBN 978-1-959986-32-4 (hardcover)
ISBN 978-1-959986-33-1 (ebook)

Library of Congress Control Number: 2026904728

Publisher's Cataloging-in-Publication
(Provided by Cassidy Cataloguing Services, Inc.)
Names: D'Agincourt, Maryann, author.
Title: Stirrings / Maryann D'Agincourt.
Description: New York : Portmay Press, [2026]
Identifiers: LCCN: 2026904728 | ISBN: 9781959986324 (hardback) | 9781959986317 (paperback) | 9781959986331 (ebook/ePub)
Subjects: LCSH: Young men--Family relationships. | Families. | Interpersonal relations. | Trust. | New York (N.Y.) | LCGFT: Domestic fiction. | BISAC: FICTION / General. | FICTION / Literary.
Classification: LCC: PS3604.A332544 S75 2026 | DDC: 813/.6--dc23

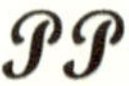

Portmay Press
244 Madison Avenue
New York, NY 10016
www.portmaypress.com

Also by Maryann D'Agincourt

Journal of Eva Morello

All Most

Glimpses of Gauguin

Printz

Shade and Light

Marriage of the Smila-Hoffmans

Midsummer

I need to feel the excitement of life stirring around me, and I will always need to feel that.

—*Pierre-Auguste Renoir*

I

Fourteen years ago, early June:

Alone in the waiting area outside his father's office, he hears muted voices—flat, disconnected—coming from the inner room. Noon light filters through half-opened blinds, warming his broad forehead, etched brows. More pensive than impatient today—unusual for a person of his age and temperament. Active. Observant.

This change in him, not missed by his mother, who for the past while has been wistful herself. Ten minutes before, she told him she needed to speak to his father. Her hand pressing his shoulder, she asked him to wait, her perfume sweet and strong. Then she turned to open the door of the private office. Sunlight played with the swirls in her short dark hair, revealing a hint of auburn.

His hands loose on his lap, he eyes the copy of the Van Gogh painting on the wall. A man and woman, arms linked, standing in the woods, staring down at him. The intense, harsh lines in the work irk him. And he thinks instead of the copy of the Winslow Homer painting in his father's study at home: Two boys of approximately his age, twelve, sitting in a pasture. It leads him to a windy April day, two months before, his mother, father, and himself, at the art museum in Boston; with one hand pressing her waist, her voice rich, modulated, his mother announced she did not like the Homer, that she found the work static, boring. He and his parents had driven down from their home in Harrington, New Hampshire that morning.

His father's response was prompt—he did not believe the work still at all. There was much stirring in those two young boys. Longings. Fears. Just beginning to evolve. Then his father moved closer to the painting, pointing out the uneasy expression of one subject and the tension in the tightly clasped hands and arched foot of the other.

Before exiting the museum, they stopped in the shop on the first floor where his father purchased a framed copy of the painting. Then they strolled toward their car parked on the Fenway, his mother and father holding hands, a wide space between their forms. The strain between his parents inside the museum annoyed him.

After spending the night in a Copley Square hotel, they returned to Harrington the next day. Soon afterward his father hung the copy of the Winslow Homer work in his home office.

Lowering his head, he now studies the swirling pattern stitched into the green oriental rug at his feet, mulling over the different iterations of his name. Though Nathaniel is his given name, his parents call him Ned, while to his friends and others of his age, he is Nate. There's a smoothness to Nate. He views himself as definite, yet gliding.

A contained excitement stirs within him, similar to a sensation he's experienced while anticipating a new bicycle or publication of the latest novel in an adventure series. But this feeling is different; for the first time, there is no cause for it—it just lingers.

His parents are a mystery to him, shadowy. He likes to envision his father on a summer evening, dressed in his off-white linen suit, and how in a sure-footed way he'll walk up the front steps of their home. His father's eyes are smiling, his mouth set. He understands his father worries—about his work, about his mother, about him.

When his father is in his home office, Nate will walk past the door, peek inside, and see his dad at his desk, furrowing his brow, perusing a history book. His father has told him he prefers to read about revolutionary wars.

Turning his thoughts to his mother, he pictures her in her room on the second floor, practicing her lines in her rich, sometimes hesitant voice. She is an actress but isn't on television or in the movies. She performs only on stage. During rehearsals, which sometimes Nate will attend, the man she calls Sam, her director, will rest his hand on his mother's waist and walk her to another part of the stage. He will brush aside a stray hair, then caress her face. Nate understands Sam is pleased with how well she understands the character she is playing, his mother has explained.

He is aware his father admires his mother more than anyone. This both comforts and puzzles him.

He was born in New York in the late 1990s. The hospital was across town from the one-bedroom apartment on 54th Street where he lived with his parents until their move, two years later, to Harrington. He was named Nathaniel Alexander Forester. Alexander had been strongly suggested by his maternal grandmother, whose family, generations before, supposedly had had ties to the Russian aristocracy.

Twenty-six now, he has no memories of those beginning years, but deep and scattered recollections of his emotions. Profound joy. Sadness. Frustration. More intense feelings than he's experienced since.

He vaguely recalls jumping onto a pile of leaves, his knees scraping against the concrete. He was four then. And at the same age, the unrestrained desire of chasing after a robin in his Harrington backyard. A cold spray of water from a rough ocean wave breaking on the New Hampshire coast.

All he knows of his first two years of life is what he has seen in a photograph of himself at eighteen months, walking up an avenue in Midtown between his parents, each holding on to one of his hands. His parents appear younger, though their bearings and expressions are the same—his mother's evoking a warm irony, his father's a mix of sensitivity and abstraction.

A young Nate would drive with his parents from Harrington to New York to visit his grandmother. While his parents were in another room, she'd take him aside and repeat the story of her family history. He'd look into her steely gaze and listen to her with the same healthy disbelief he would a fairytale. Yet he was drawn to her imagination—insistent and forthright.

His maternal grandmother, a distinguished-looking woman with dark eyes and hair pulled back in a severe yet becoming style, was a few inches taller than his mother. His grandparent's build was sturdy in comparison to her daughter's. She wore high heels no matter the time of day or occasion. His maternal grandfather and grandmother had divorced years before he was born. Soon afterward she had married a solid-looking man with a background similar to hers, who liked the best wines and cigars, and who, unlike her former husband, granted her and himself much freedom.

While his parents traveled, Nate would spend time alone with his grandmother in her New York apartment, and often she would bring him to a Russian restaurant with red leather seats. On certain occasions her husband would accompany them, but mostly it was the two of them. Entering the restaurant, holding on to his grandmother's firm hand, inhaling her tangy perfume, he would hear sounds of laughter and music. They would sit in the same booth at the back of the restaurant, close to the small round stage where an instrumentalist would perform. His grandmother would hand Nate her glass. He'd take one sip of vodka. Once he had done so, she would commend him for making the effort, then swiftly pat him on the back; she knew he found vodka as distasteful as an unpleasant medicine.

After they ordered, the owner would join them, and would sit close to his grandmother, brushing against her. And the staff would treat Nate as if they'd always known him.

As he matured, he began to realize the joking rapport between his grandmother and the owner of the restaurant could have been masking a sexual attraction. And when he was much older and no longer needed to stay with his grandmother, it would occur to him every now and again that his grandmother may have been having an affair with this man, whose name he could not recall.

His parents would leave him with his grandmother and her husband in August when they'd spend two or three weeks in Europe. He liked the homemade blintzes his grandmother made, that she'd wear a dress in the kitchen without donning an apron. But what he liked most about her was her overall presence, strong, seemingly invincible, unwavering. It wasn't that he found his mother uncertain, but there was a subtle hesitation in her that he had been aware of since he was a young child. Intuitively, he understood his mother was an adventurous person, but she also was fearful.

* * *

He was aware his parents had met in New York and that his father, a psychiatrist, had, after completing his training, moved down from Boston to distance himself from his own father's career in the same profession.

Although his paternal grandparents eventually had moved to Europe and then passed before he had met them, he knew—it was as if he always had—that his grandfather and his father were very different from each other. How he had come to be aware of this? Sometimes he'd wonder if he had been born with this knowledge.

When his parents were not home and he was old enough to be alone for a few hours, he'd go into his father's office and open the closet door, where there was a cardboard box on the floor filled with photographs. He'd drag the box out onto the rug before his father's desk. At the bottom of the box there were newspaper clippings, which he did not read until he was in his mid-teens.

He'd sit on the cold floor, and pull out pictures of his paternal grandparents, holding each photo up to the light. With intense curiosity he'd study each one in detail. His father's mother was narrow and small with fine features and light red hair like his father's. His grandfather had the same set mouth as his father, but there was something about him that caused Nate to feel uneasy. Nate understood that he would forever be a mystery to him. After thorough examinations of the pictures over a number of years, Nate decided he would not follow the same profession as his father. He would not be able to help people—he'd only confuse them more. His temperament was different from his father's—he was more of a free spirit, even more so than his mother.

* * *

At twenty-six, what he most likes to recall is the evening he had exerted his independence. A cold early December day, he was six months short of thirteen.

The door of his father's home office was partly open. Nate walked in without knocking. He stood close for a few minutes. Soon his father raised his head and looked over. Stephen's eyes were red, his shoulders hunched. He studied his son for a moment. "What would you like, Ned?"

"I want you to call me Nate."

His father lowered his head and was silent. Then, gazing over at his son, he asked, "Your mother too?"

Nate nodded.

"This decision is yours—it is who you are, who you want to be."

Nate turned around and left the room. Justified. Elated.

A few days later, he was on his way out the door to play basketball at the gym, his mother came up to him; crossing her arms, she said that his father was a very serious person, he needed to have time alone, that he should not be disturbed unless necessary. Nate avoided her gaze. Over the past four months, he had been angry with her, had not been able to look her in the eye or trust her words.

"He's different from me and maybe from you—though you are young yet, Ned, I mean Nate. You may change and become more like your father, or maybe you'll be like neither of us, which is the best," she added. She spoke frankly, though he heard doubt in her voice.

Early May, unseasonable, a cold musky rain falls. Nate peers out through a window of the bookstore. Water pounds the sidewalk, forming rivulets along Broadway. A rainstorm in Harrington, same time of year, crosses his mind. His thoughts then slide to the day he sat waiting for his mother outside his father's office. It was when he began to comprehend the adult world was not what it seemed.

At the time there were only the three of them, his parents and himself. The school year was coming to a close. He was anticipating summer, endless hours with nothing to do, warm weather, riding his scooter alongside his closest friend, exchanging few words, a soft breeze enfolding them.

Whenever he believes his life may devolve into chaos, he'll

turn to that June day, fourteen years ago, as one will seek a close friend, a relative, or read a favored philosopher's writings, or, for those with spiritual leanings, scripture.

Edging closer to the entrance of the bookstore, he reaches inside the pocket of his raincoat, feels something soft, and pulls out a face mask—he cannot remember when he last used it. The pandemic seems so long ago, then again, it is as if it were yesterday.

He walks back again to the window and peers out, studying the slanting angle of the rain. Two nights before, rain slapping the windowpanes of his apartment, Adrianna, without saying a word, got up from the bed and began to pack her belongings.

Many times over the past month she had spoken to him about his inability to be emotionally present, her dark hair falling across her eyes. She'd twist her mouth to the side in a heartfelt way. Then she'd add that she might be wrong, maybe she was the absent one—it was difficult to be certain; the isolation during the virus had caused her to question herself more, even after it was over.

And now he wonders if, as the rain pelted the apartment windows that night, it had struck her that it was him, not her. But she did not mention it when she left; she quietly closed the door behind her as he lay paralyzed on the bed.

She still rented an apartment with three others in Williamsburg. Adrianna and he would meet at this bookstore after work every evening. He'd look forward to her walking in, carrying a bag, the handle over her wrist—inside would be a pastry for each of them.

They first met the summer before the pandemic. Both were still in college, vacationing in Italy, each with a group from their respective school. He noticed her standing alone at the bottom of the Spanish Steps. He assumed she was an Italian; she resembled the women of Rome. When he saw an apprehensive expression cross her face, her top lip raised, he approached her. As he came closer, he understood this was not her country, that mostly likely she was an American; it was how she was dressed, blue jeans and a black halter top. A designer's name in silver lettering across the left pocket of her pants.

He spoke in English, asked if she was looking for someone. Briefly she met his gaze and nodded. Pointing behind her, he said, "The Spanish Steps. Are we in Italy?" A slight smile began to cross her lips. Then a woman towering over Adrianna came up to them, a friend of hers, he assumed. He moved away.

During that trip, the two college groups once dined together at a restaurant near Piazza Navona; they sat across the room from each other, a glowing candle on the table before her. The soft light covered her slanting cheekbones, small face. Nate nearly caught her gaze, but she turned away to speak to the person next to her. They did not become a couple until later—they met again by chance during the pandemic, at a grocery store in his neighborhood.

Again, he recalls that June day, fourteen years before, and how the summer did not evolve as he had hoped, a few months later his friend moved away, and the relationship between his mother, father, and himself began to unravel.

His thoughts turn to Adrianna. At any moment she may walk through the door with treats in her bag. It is unlikely—he is not in love with her. A sense of loss. A longing. Hopeful and darkly uncertain, he looks towards the entrance. Is she coming though the doorway? Is it Adrianna?

Fourteen years ago, I knew of Nate Forester. I, Lainie Moreau, following the unexpected death of my father, had moved to Harrington, New Hampshire, to stay with my aunt Laura and her husband. Until then, I had been living with my family in a suburb south of Boston. It was a mixed community, unlike the freshly painted homes and manicured lawns of Harrington. Our family home was a cape, small and cluttered, with a front lawn and no backyard. The color of the home was difficult to determine—gray or brown—due to exposure to the harsh New England weather. My two older brothers slept in the same bedroom, and I had the narrow room next to the kitchen.

At the time of my father's passing, my brothers were working their way through college, attending university on a part-time basis. And I would begin high school that fall.

My mother had needed space to mourn, to collect herself, to find employment. She thought if I stayed for a period of time with her sister, it would be beneficial to the both of us. She would be free to grieve openly without worrying about the effect her mood would have on me. As her sister's home was an hour and twenty minutes from hers, she was able to visit me regularly. And when she did, she'd tightly embrace me, her smile hopeful.

My aunt and her husband, having chosen not to have children, were an independent couple. My living with them for this time seemed of no consequence—I did not disrupt their lifestyle. If both needed to go out for the night—my aunt to meet a friend or her husband to have dinner with his colleagues from work—I was old enough to stay on my own.

Before my father's passing, our family life had been predictable. During the summer, we would spend much of the day at the beach, which was a little less than two miles from our home. In the late afternoon, we'd return home to play or mingle with our friends in the neighborhood until we were called in to dinner.

On hot nights we'd be out on a neighbor's front lawn or our own, listening to the murmuring voices of our parents and the parents of our friends coming from inside the home of the family who happened to be hosting that evening. When it became dark, we'd recognize one another only by the light beaming from the flashlights we carried. We all got along well, but my father's sudden passing changed everything. People became suspicious of one another—for no reason other than a deep distrust of loss. I was relieved when my mother sent me to live with her sister in New Hampshire. I needed a break from our life, which had been transformed from an existence fueled by a gritty optimism to one burning with doubt and confusion.

* * *

I arrived in Harrington on an afternoon in late July. When I stepped out of my mother's dark blue Toyota, I felt the dryness in the air. The sun was overbearing. The leaves on the tress appeared listless. Though I had visited my aunt and her husband before, I understood that my life was different now.

A few days later, Nadine, the daughter of my aunt's neighbor, knocked on the door, invited herself in. We spoke for a long while. Her first words to me were, "I'm sorry about your father—I would hate to lose mine." We were the same age. Then she squeezed my hand, and said, "I will be your guide to Harrington."

Nadine and I were opposite in appearance and temperament. She was slightly below average height, not plump but round and attractive. She was fair-skinned and her hair a dark blond color, her eyes a warm brown. I, on the other hand, was an inch taller than she was, and slight, my eyes gray-green.

While I was withdrawn—I had been this way even before my father passed—she was open and giving to people who needed someone to lift them up. Yet despite our different approaches to the world, we were surprisingly compatible.

A week before school started, I spent a night at Nadine's home. Her tone more serious than usual, she told me about Nate Forester and his family. Sitting out on the front top step, a hint of fall in the air, she said that the Foresters were known because Nate's mother was an actress. She performed at the theater by the sea. Although Harrington was a small city, people came from different parts of New England, and sometimes from Canada, to attend this well-respected theater. Had I heard of it? she asked, turning to me. Before I could answer, she mentioned in an off-hand way that in the past Nate's mother had been an actress on the New York stage.

A few days later Nadine and I were walking down Main Street, on our way to shop for school supplies at Woolworth's. Suddenly she stopped. She pointed out Nate to me. He was across the street, alone, on a scooter. He seemed much younger than us, even though, according to Nadine, it was only a one-year age difference. I shrugged, feigning indifference. But I had been struck by his presence, his vulnerability. More focused on starting school in a new place, not wanting to be diverted by people younger than I was, I pushed aside thoughts of Nate.

During the school year I would notice Nate walking across the street or sitting beneath a tree with his scooter resting against the trunk. Sometimes he'd be coming out of a restaurant with one or two adults, who I had assumed were his parents. He seemed to be alone most of the time. If I happened to be with Nadine, she no longer pointed him out. At first I thought he was no longer of interest to her, but then realized he might never have been—mentioning Nate and his family may have been her way of introducing me to Harrington.

During the school year, Nadine and I were inseparable. She was quite popular and I was included in her circle of friends. It was a new world for me. In my previous school my friends were not very social. Most were young women of my age, and occasionally a male or two would become part of our small gathering, but would never stay long.

Nadine's friends were of both sexes. And I was convinced that if Nadine had not been my aunt's neighbor, I would not have belonged to this group.

We would choose different partners to socialize with, but it was acceptable; there was no outward anger or jealousy. Young, good-natured, and curious, our purpose was to experiment, to learn about life.

Using makeup and suggesting an appropriate hairstyle, Nadine taught me how to hide the red scar on the left side of my face—it was close to the shape of an arrow. Without any makeup or hair covering it, the red line was narrow but dark and noticeable. For the first time, I was considered attractive. Savoring the attention, I continued to follow Nadine's instructions on how to camouflage my scar.

* * *

When my mother visited, she was exhausted—it took a lot of energy for her to piece her life back together. Her visits reassured me that I was still part of her life. I began to understand it was why I had been moved by Nate—he was as alone as I was.

The following spring our English teacher took us to the theater where Nate's mother performed. We saw Shakespeare's *Romeo and Juliet*, the play we were reading in class. Nate's mother was Juliet's mother, Lady Capulet.

It was an unseasonably hot April day. Just before intermission, I squeezed out from my seat, hoping to avoid the rush to the concession stand. I was very thirsty. As I made my way up the aisle, I saw Nate's mother standing a few feet away, under an awning, in front of a fan. A man came up behind her, sidling close to her, he began rubbing her arms. "Stop it," she cried out. Her voice was harsh. "It's too hot for that sort of thing." Abruptly, she turned to him, kissed him hard and briefly on the mouth, then swiftly walked away, her Lady Capulet dress swishing.

I thought of Nate, who appeared young and gentle. I was intrigued, though my interest in the Foresters eventually subsided. I can't recall coming across Nate or his mother again. It was as if he had disappeared from Harrington.

Yet I am not certain I did not see him again—it was some years ago.

* * *

A year later I returned to my home in the Boston area. My aunt would call from time to time. Once I had my driver's license, we'd meet halfway between our homes for lunch on a Saturday. Because she had been kind to me, had taken me in at a poignant time in my life, I was happy to oblige her.

During our lunch get-togethers, it was clear that my aunt was hoping to learn something from me. And after so many meetings when I did not provide her with any significant information, she stopped contacting me.

It took me years to realize what it was she had needed to know.

I dream of Aunt Laura—she's running. Panting. It is night. Her legs move with Atalanta-like speed, her arms flailing. The reflection of the street lights brightly crossing her form, her face is narrower, bony, her expression fearful. In the morning, still shaken from the dream, I open my eyes to a ray of sun streaming into my bedroom.

This hot July afternoon, I drive the sixty-plus miles north on Route 95 to visit my aunt—it's been five years since we were last together. A warmer than usual New England summer, I pass clusters of dry leafy trees bordering the highway. Nearly thirteen years have passed since I left Harrington.

Turning onto the street, I spot my aunt's place, two down on the right. I pull up in front. Her home is smaller than I remember. I walk up the cement pathway of the old gray Victorian, the porch still seeming small for the size of the house. Five feet from the stairs, I remember how uneven they were, and soon see they have not been repaired.

I spot her through an open window, her back facing me. For a moment she seems a stranger. Standing in front of the mirror in the foyer, her shoulders erect, she's fluffing her hair. Then she slightly turns her head to the side. She's expecting someone—how she's assessing her appearance, the edgy movement of her shoulders.

Without warning she opens the door and a look of mild disappointment crosses her face, but then she catches herself and smile openly, welcoming me, her arms wide. As she embraces me, I apologize for not calling first. Ignoring my words, she guides me into the sitting room. I am flooded with memories of doing homework on the floor late at night, the television on with the sound off; and how every so often I would steal a glimpse at the screen.

My aunt serves me coffee, and then we sit out on the porch. We rock in our chairs, but not in synchrony. The sun goes behind the clouds and it appears quieter. I look across the front yard and think how much smaller it seems. When I was here last I was fifteen, a half-inch shorter than I am now.

* * *

There is silence except for the sound of our chairs rocking over the wooden flooring. The sun emerges from behind a white fluffy cloud, stronger than before. My aunt appears lost in thought.

Abruptly she rocks forward and then stops, turns her head to me, I meet her gray gaze. She asks if I remember the Forester family. Her eyes are now darting. I feel jarred to hear the name spoken out in the open. My memories of Nate had been private. I'd not spoken of him to anyone other than those few times with Nadine. A vague image comes to mind of Nate sitting alone under a tree, a scooter resting against the trunk. He appeared sad, unhappy. I had been drawn to him. But I do not recall if I was alone or with someone else or exactly when this was.

I look over at my aunt. "I see you remember," she says, and smiles lightly. "They no longer live in Harrington." She pauses and runs one finger over the slope of the armrest. "They moved away five years ago, though I believe their son left before they did. They were odd in that they were living in Harrington, but didn't belong here. It was said that the actress had had an affair with her director—supposedly a short-lived one, and that her husband wasn't angry about it in the least. People were not surprised about the affair—it was inevitable, working so closely as they did. There were those who questioned her husband, wondered if he did not care. He seemed to carry on with his life, no change in him."

"Gossip," I say, and look away, thinking how Nate had been a diversion for me. What else did I have those early months in Harrington? I was a lonely young person in an unfamiliar place. My friends did not count as we were a very public group. I was longing for privacy.

"Maybe her husband hid his feelings because he was not able to share them. He didn't know how to." I hear a slight tension in my voice.

She smiles at me as if I am naive. "I don't know how well you are aware of the family," she adds.

"I don't know the family at all, really."

"I had a close friend at the time you lived with us. I don't know if you remember her—tall, dark hair, dignified. Emotion in her eyes. Stephen Forester was her psychiatrist. From what she said at the time, it crossed my mind that he may have been infatuated with her. But she trusted him, so maybe I am wrong."

"I don't recall her," I say easily.

"She lived in Harrington with her husband for only a year—they were here because of his work. You might not have met her."

I shrug and rock some more, thinking of how I'd go out on errands with my aunt. It was a slow, meandering process; my aunt would walk close to me, turn her head in my direction and make a comment as if confiding in me alone.

Yet now I see there is more to my aunt, she may have another life I know nothing about. As I sit next to her rocking, I close my eyes and try to remember if there were any signs of her behavior that seemed out of character during the time I lived with her and her husband. As I was in high school, I was self-focused—I never really thought of her as an individual. I took it for granted that she was calm, unflappable—it was what I needed at the time. I never questioned why she and her husband were often apart. Where each of them went on their nights out I was never certain. I was not aware how late either of them returned. It might have been in the early morning, before I awakened.

I appreciated being with Aunt Laura—her presence ameliorated my deep sense of loss. I was living in another world, a world without the reality of a grieving mother, two tense and hardworking older brothers, a deceased father. Instead it was one with vague forms entering and exiting my aunt and uncle's home. No rules. I could come and go as I pleased—a never-ending dream without substance or direction. There is much about that time I do not recall.

A stifling August morning. Distinct sounds of humming rouse Nate from his sleep. A rock piece with classical undertones. Hazily he searches his memory for the name of the song. Carrying a tray with two cups of coffee and pastries, Adrianna kicks open the bedroom door. Her white silk robe is open, the belt dangling. Her eyes still heavy with sleep. She moves her head to the rhythm of the song, more at ease when humming the classical elements. She has told Nate she had years of piano lessons, which on certain days she enjoyed—she had hoped to become a concert pianist—and at other times she resented, the endless hours of practice.

He catches her gaze and smiles. She shrugs, her hair splaying across her shoulders.

* * *

Adrianna understood she was a part of New York; she had lived there all her life. She did not know where her personality ended and that of the city began. That night three months ago when she had left Nate in the middle of a rainstorm she had had no concerns. Her friend had been there to pick her up. What she regretted was not explaining her abrupt departure to Nate. She hadn't been aware of what it was that had compelled her to leave without an explanation. She had never been a silent person. It was as if she had been in a trance.

She concluded that the ethical thing to do would be to return to Nate, to acknowledge that the discussions they had had over the previous month had led to incomprehension on his part and silence. But still it wasn't about Nate's reaction or lack of one, it was about her identity—it wasn't in her nature to be irresponsible. After completing her work in the children's room of the library that rainy May day, she walked out onto the sidewalk, opened her umbrella and hastened to the bookstore. To lessen her expectation, she assumed Nate would not be there.

Opening the door, she closed her umbrella, shook it and felt a splash of water cross her wrist. She lifted her head and spotted Nate looking toward the entrance. She rested her gaze on him before he noticed her. She saw that he was uneasy. It then struck her that he was waiting for her and she felt a stab of delight.

Nate believed he simply had imagined her coming in. There were many people moving through the door now. No longer could he find the person he thought was Adrianna. He decided to leave. Moving toward the exit, he felt a tug on his sleeve.

* * *

No longer humming, Adrianna easily places the tray on Nate's lap. Then she takes off her robe, dropping it onto the floor. She gets into bed, sidles close to him; she reaches for a cup of coffee, her hair falling across his chest.

They have spent more time apart than together these past three months. They each understand something is missing, something is unsaid between them. There is an empty space separating them that they try to bridge but are inept at doing so.

They spend this Saturday lying in bed, the air conditioning unit jammed in the open window, on full blast, the half-empty breakfast tray on the floor at the foot of the bed. She is reading *A Portrait of the Artist as a Young Man* for the third time. His computer screen to his right, he now and again watches the Yankees play the Dodgers, the sound on mute. A sketch pad on his lap, he is working on a drawing of one of the children he instructs at the hospital, a young boy with dark hair, a long nose, and hopeful eyes.

He feels Adrianna looking at his picture. He turns to her and says, "I am not an artist. I don't want to be. I just draw."

Studying the sketch more, she eyes him, and says, "You may be better than most." He takes her hand and kisses it, then lowering his head he presses his lips to her bare shoulder, senses the quickening of her heart.

* * *

They wait until five in the afternoon before they venture out into the city.

Over appetizers at the café a few blocks from Nate's apartment, they sip wine in silence. Adrianna pushes back her hair, which overpowers her face, her chin too narrow, her eyes now closing.

Her passionate nature is in conflict with her need to think logically—he has comprehended this about her for a while. It is what he admires most about her.

"Adrianna—it's summer," he says, knowing she may resent the lightness in his tone.

She takes a sip of wine and shrugs. "I won't bring up anything unpleasant." She looks up at the sky, her eyes misty. "It will be a beautiful night. We can take a long walk."

"The beach tomorrow?" he suggests.

She nods and looks away from him.

He reaches for her hand.

She refuses to meet his gaze. His first instinct is to withdraw his grasp but he stops himself—he isn't going to give in so easily. She has been waiting for him to be annoyed with her, and when he isn't, she accepts his mood, his persevering nature.

He believes what she wants to say is that after three months of trying, their relationship may no longer exist. He does not want to hear it on this day, at this hour. He acknowledges there is an empty space between them—but they are groping toward each other, hoping to cross the vacuum, waiting to come upon something real, visceral about the other.

Six weeks have passed since I visited my aunt in Harrington. Because of a job transfer, I left Massachusetts a month ago and moved to southern Connecticut. I sent an email to my aunt to let her know of my move and new address. She has not called or sent me an email or text in response.

In my new apartment, the first floor of a Victorian home with a spacious porch and long windows, the early September light is quite beautiful, how it falls across the bedroom in the morning. The house is painted an off-white color, and my living area has recently been refurbished—high ceilings, and walls a light peach.

Late afternoon, a cup of coffee in hand, I gaze out past the glass French doors and watch the late summer sun begin its descent. Faint light splashes the floor, the wood an apricot color now.

In the hallway, a row of unpacked boxes diminishes the loveliness of the moment. I go over and begin to take out books. Soon I stop. I have had a long week at work and want to enjoy the stillness and quiet of evening.

I am still learning what is expected, and about the personalities of my colleagues. Although when in Boston much of my work was done remotely, it was necessary for me to move to the Connecticut office as there are many projects occurring here. They need me in Connecticut, my expertise, which has to do with holding group meetings allowing people to express their ideas, bringing out the best in people. It is what I am known for in terms of my career—bringing out the best in people, creatively, personally. It moves along a project. Yet in my relationships with men I have attempted to bring out the best in each one but once they realize it, they resent me.

There was Tim—I met him on my day off at a burger place in Boston. It was early spring and still cold. He was eating at the high-top table next to mine. It was crowded, people dressed in bulky winter clothing were devouring burgers in a small area. I had errands to do and I was in as much of a rush as everyone else. I felt a foot on mine and looked up. Tim apologized profusely and blushed. "No worries," I said, but he remained red-faced and I tried to say something to make him feel comfortable. "It is nice of you to apologize, I usually don't," I added. He then smiled. I wasn't certain if I had made him feel at ease or if he was amused. He had a flushed complexion and very high short lines for eyebrows, his face much too round, no sense of definition, though his still physique was consoling. It is what drew me to him.

We were together for six months, and separated once it struck him that he was too dependent on me. I had encouraged him to look for another job, one where his abilities would be more appreciated. Eventually he told me he was fine where he was. He did not want more from life than what he had achieved, which he was pleased with more than I could imagine.

One night, a month before we broke up, we were in bed. I lay in his arms, his chest broad but soft, he told me that I liked giving advice, but I didn't talk much about myself, that I kept my distance, that I did not want to be known.

These last two years, since Tim, I have been cautious of stepping into another relationship based on one miscommunication or another. I wonder if I should not be involved with anyone, if my personality is not suited to it, if essentially I am a loner.

I think of my aunt living her life away in that old house with her husband. Neither seeming to connect with those who entered their home.

Her husband is an avid golfer. But I never really knew him. He just went in and out of the house. I was never quite certain what he did for work. Each morning he left home dressed in a shirt and tie and he'd nod at me. He would return at the end of the day with his tie off and the top two buttons of his shirt undone. And he would nod at me for the second time that day.

My aunt appeared unfazed by his long absences playing golf. I do not believe I ever witnessed them kissing or holding hands. They were not an affectionate couple, but not everyone has to be. I remember my parents were sometimes affectionate and sometimes not, but there seemed to be a bond between them that didn't exist between my aunt and her husband.

Once I saw them exchange a gaze. It was during one of my mother's visits. She was talking about my father as if he were alive. My uncle and aunt eyed one another, wondering, I believed, if she was delusional. I was angry. I thought my mother had a right to speak of my father in any way she wished. She was still in mourning. I knew she was not unstable. I saw my uncle and aunt in a different light; I had not thought of them until then as judgmental—they seemed beyond that. I understood that they viewed themselves as immune to rules and conventions. They proceeded with their lives as they chose and were not concerned about how gracious or not they were. They were not kind people.

I wanted to leave them that day, but something prevented me from doing so. I can't remember why. Maybe it was because of a call my aunt received from someone. I do not remember who. It seemed to cause her much worry, and the conversation switched at that moment. For some reason, which I can't recall, we now were focused solely on my aunt, her concerns.

My cell phone rings once, a clanging sound. I am dining with someone I met in the Connecticut office. Craig. He has fine dark hair, parted on the left, an olive complexion and pale blue eyes. His brows are narrow, and the expression in his eyes is beguiling at times, off-putting at others. He is inscrutable. I have resisted accepting his invitation for nearly two weeks.

We are drinking wine, have been talking of places we have traveled, which type of movies we like, our favorite ones, and then the conversation turns to our work. "You were transferred from the Boston office because you bring out the best in your colleagues, I hear. I guess they think no one in Connecticut is capable of doing so," he says with a brief laugh.

I smile, not certain if he is teasing me or is annoyed. Before

I have a chance to respond, my phone rings again, more than once now. I apologize and take my phone from my jacket pocket. As I put it on a silent mode, I see the call is coming in from Harrington, New Hampshire. I hesitate, look across the table, meeting his gaze.

"Take it. You look as if it is important."

"Yes," I tell him, "it may be. Do you mind if I go outside?"

He seems mildly disappointed, but tells me to go ahead and do what I think is best.

Ten minutes later, I return to the table, and he says that I look like I've seen a ghost. His voice is direct but noncommittal.

I tell him that I have heard disappointing news. I am not certain if it is true. It is not clear.

He nods and calls for the waiter. He orders me a whiskey. "Hopefully, this will help," he says with a half-smile. I take a long sip of the drink. A burning sensation. Not accustomed to liquor, I am unsteady.

The call was from Aunt Laura's husband; he told me that she had left him. He sounded confused. I asked him if he had contacted my mother, suggested she might know about her sister's whereabouts. But he hung up before I finished speaking. It was odd.

I look over at Craig. He is studying me. Taking another sip of whiskey, I touch my face, the scar, wondering if I may have wiped away my makeup.

He tells me he is from Chicago, born there. He continues to observe the scar on my face, now with a soft curiosity. Tears spring to my eyes. Rarely do I cry. The whiskey. I collect myself, refusing to be revealed to someone I do not know.

It is a quiet night, not many cars on the road. One hand on the steering wheel, Craig is a casual driver, a Midwesterner. Other than pleasantries—the beautiful early fall evening, how soon the temperature will drop—we do not speak. It is a short drive. He stops in front of my home. Slipping out of the car, I turn, lower my head, and wave good-bye. Once I am inside my apartment, I look out the window. He has not driven away. I go into the bedroom, undress, and put on my blue robe. Then I go to the front window and check again. He is still there. He has been parked outside for about twenty minutes.

I take a long shower. Then I wrap a towel around my head. Again, I don my robe. I go to the sofa in the next room, pick up the remote control, and click the on button. I don't look at the television screen. I am thinking of my conversation with my aunt's husband. Unusual. It is difficult to believe my aunt would have left him. Was he drunk?

Exhausted, I doze off. I dream I am alone in a large and unfamiliar house. I am lost and cannot find my way out. I believe the exit is in the room I am in, but is it in the next one or the one after that? I go from one room to the next, but so far the exit door is not in any one of them. I become more and more anxious. Then I hear a knock on a door, and follow the sound—it may be the door that will lead me out. The knock is strong. I wake up and realize I am no longer dreaming.

Abruptly I get up, then hear a thump—the remote control

has fallen to the floor. I make my way to the foyer and open the door. I stand back, then turn away. He comes up behind me, embracing me, kissing the side of my face, my scar, insistently. Under his breath, he asks, "Why?" He loosens the belt of my robe. I sway, nearly losing my balance, then shrug it off.

II

A warm late September day, weeks before foliage will peak. Along the sidewalk, a scattering of leaves are beginning to turn a pale yellow, a light red. Nate, uneasy, approaches the building where his parents live. He doesn't know what their mood will be.

Pete, the doorman, pacing before the entrance way, stops and greets Nate. They talk briefly about the Yankees, the baseball season.

Opening the glass door to the building, Pete raises his face to the sun.

The woman behind the reception desk, her thick red hair pulled back in an elastic band, smiles and nods at Nate.

The elevator doors open to an empty lift. Nate presses the button to floor 10. His thoughts wander aimlessly, amorphous at one moment, specific at the next, never connecting. He wonders if he is losing his sense of gravity.

The doors slide open. Stepping out of the elevator, he looks to the left and down the wide hallway, notices a woman leaving his parents' apartment. She does not glance in his direction. They pass in the hallway. Apparently preoccupied with her thoughts, she appears unaware of him, of his presence.

Turning, he watches her walk in an even, forward-moving way toward the elevator. She has a scar—a narrow one, unusual—like an arrow on the side of her face. Etched on her cheek with purpose and precision? Familiar, he thinks; within seconds his impression dissipates.

Quietly, he turns the knob, opening the door to the apartment. His parents are deep in conversation. His mother, seated on the arm of the sofa, her shoulders hunched forward, leafing through a magazine while speaking. The afternoon light covering her face discloses lines surrounding her eyes, deeper now. She has aged some, he realizes. He visits her every few weeks and has not noticed until now. She resembles his grandmother more. He feels a loss for what has once been, his mother's energetic beauty, her hesitant optimism, and then the other side of her. Demanding. Passionate.

His father, reclining in an armchair across from his mother, a closed computer on his lap, studies her as she speaks, his lips parting.

They end their conversation once they see he has let himself in. His mother catches his gaze and smiles warmly, briefly. His father eyes him readily, pleased to see him.

“You’ve had a visitor?” Nate asks, sitting at the other end of the sofa from his mother. He leans forward and picks up the oversized art book on Matisse from the coffee table. He studies each page before moving on to the next one, more captivated by the images than he is interested in his mother or father’s response.

Eyeing him, his mother says, “Yes, we have. It isn’t important. She is not someone we know. She lived in Harrington once for a short time.” She looks away; he is not certain if it is because the visitor is not a person who has intrigued her, or she does not want to reveal to him who she is or why she has come to them.

His father, appearing calm, lightly taps his fingers on the arm of his chair—the only sign that he may be intrigued in some way by her visit. Though he seems more ponderous about it than worried.

“I noticed a scar on the side of her face,” Nate says. “Unusual, like an arrow. I think I saw that once on someone, but can’t remember where or when. You said she lived in Harrington?”

“It may not be a scar—it may be unevenly applied rouge,” his mother said. She springs up, goes into the bedroom and soon returns with some rouge on her face to show him.

Nate carefully looks at the streak of rouge on the side of his mother’s face and says, “It is a much narrower line than that—more narrow and darker.”

"Does it matter? You might have recognized her from Harrington—and she may or may not have a scar or rouge on her face. None of this matters. You are wondering why she was here," his father responds. He sounds guarded, Nate thinks.

"Why did she come to us, Stephen? We do not know if what she says is true. We don't know her. I have no recollection of her or of her aunt and uncle. Do you?"

Nate looks over at his father.

He shrugs and says, "I need to think it over. I met a lot of people while we were there. I can't recall everyone's name. I may know of them. I need time to refresh my memory. I am not sure."

"Well, I am certain, Stephen. I don't know them." Brea shrugs her shoulders and assertively stands up.

Nate studies his mother. He is accustomed to the sudden and dramatic way she has of expressing herself. But he is able to delve beyond her words, her affect—it usually takes him a moment or two to penetrate what her true feelings are. And as he does so now, he sees fear in her, in the movement of her lips. He looks over at his father, who does not appear to be listening to his mother. Nate supposes his mother is more upset with whatever this woman said than is his father.

Sliding the art book back onto the table, he then gets up, goes over to his mother and hugs her. As they embrace, he knows she is comforted—she believes he understands her fears. Yet there is much more he cannot comprehend about her. He is careful to hide his ambivalence. He catches his reflection in the mirror next to the door, hoping his mother does not see disappointment in his eyes. He takes a sidelong glance at his father, who has opened his computer and is reading a news article.

The late September meeting with Stephen and Brea Forester was hurried and abrupt. Though not obvious at first, both have strong personalities. I was surprised. Because of their age and worldliness, I expected a more subtle couple. Something about them blocked me from gauging them objectively—unusual—and I became uneasy.

If it wasn't for my aunt's disappearance, I would have left even earlier than I did. When it comes to seeking information about Aunt Laura I am persistent.

When I first called the Foresters, I asked if they knew of my aunt from Harrington, explained that I'd understood they had lived there for a while and that my aunt had mentioned them when I saw her last in July. They were hesitant, but agreed that if I were in New York I could stop by. They did not want to deny me—they were sorry that my aunt was missing. Their first inclination was to be gracious.

But that September day, the moment I sat down, Brea told me, her voice adamant, that they have been away from Harrington for over five years, and were uncertain why I had come to them. They had no connection to my aunt or uncle, could not recall if they had ever met, and if they had it would have been a short and superficial interaction. Harrington, she added, is a small town—people know each other without *really* knowing each other.

Stephen's silence was telling—I wasn't convinced he was in complete agreement with his wife.

My time with them ended soon after that. I was uncomfortable; I understood that they, especially Brea, viewed me as an intrusion in their lives. That had not been my intent in going to their home. Because my aunt had mentioned the family, I thought they might have some information—whether they realized it or not—that could in some way help me comprehend my aunt's disappearance.

I am hoping today will be different from the day we first met. It is the third week of October, a brisk and bright fall day, cold for this time of year. Riding the elevator to their apartment, I am flushed from the wind, my face cold.

Opening the door with a welcoming gesture, Stephen suggests that if I like the sun, I should sit on the sofa. Then he asks if I'd like a cup of coffee. It is 10 AM on a Saturday morning.

Autumn light, strong and golden, streams into the living area. Dr. Forester appears younger today—his hair is shorter than it was when I saw him last, damp, close to his head, and he is wearing blue jeans and a black sweatshirt with white lettering close together, difficult to read.

They are more subdued today. I wonder if they have checked into my background with people they may have been friendly with in Harrington. And maybe it is why they are less hesitant and more confident with me.

Brea is wearing a red sweater, her hair appears darker in contrast. Her pants are black and silk and fall gracefully on her. "Have you had breakfast?" Her voice is quiet, her manner is effortless. Then as an afterthought, she asks, "Have you found your aunt?"

"A few weeks ago my mother received a letter from her sister. She could not read the postmark and my aunt did not say where she is living. From the tone of the letter, my mother believes she may not be in danger, that she may have chosen to leave her husband, but she is not yet convinced."

Stephen comes into the room, carrying a tray with cups of coffee. He places the tray on the table, then hands me a cup. He is pleased that I have come again, he says, and that he was surprised by my last visit, adding that the news I gave them was unexpected and it brought up old memories of Harrington, some pleasant and some not. But he has searched his memory and cannot recall my aunt and uncle's names or meeting either of them.

Brea places one hand on her hip and says she understands

why I came to see them but reminders of Harrington are difficult. She apologizes if she was short with me the last time I was there. "Those years in New Hampshire were not comfortable ones," she explains, shaking her head. "We were never part of the community." She adds that they had come to the conclusion that it had not been the best decision to have brought up their son in Harrington, and for high school had sent him to a boarding school in Boston.

There is something of the fading actress about Brea, her voice rich, though slightly hesitant. She may not believe she is as much of a presence as she once was. She is not beautiful and perhaps never was. But she has a look of the thespian about her, a wide mouth, short dark hair, revealing a full oval-shaped face. Her warm brown eyes at times appear dazed and at other moments penetrating.

She tells me that although her husband retired from his practice when they left Harrington, he still does consulting work on a part-time basis at a hospital in New York. And she still performs from time to time in the theater, but only when she finds a role that suits her. Her husband does not speak very much.

Brea comes over to me, puts her hand on my shoulder and asks, "What brought you to Harrington? Why did you stay for such a short time?"

I explain that my father had passed away and my mother had sent me there to stay with her sister—my aunt—and her husband.

"I wish I had known your aunt as I—we—would like to help you."

Brea turns away. I meet Stephen's gaze.

"You are from Massachusetts," he says affirmatively.

"Yes, I live in Connecticut now."

Brea, standing before the window, crosses her arms. Defiant. Sunlight in her eyes, she doesn't flinch. Stephen sits back in his chair, smiling, his mouth closed.

I break the silence: "I believe I told you the last time I was here that my aunt spoke of your family when I visited her last July. I'd not seen her in years. She wanted to make a point about knowing you, asking if I remembered the Forester family. I thought there was more behind her question, that she was connected to the two of you in some way."

Stephen lowers his head. Brea turns to me and asks, her voice direct, "What did you say?"

"I told her that I knew of your son Nate, that he was a year younger than I was, that I don't believe I'd ever spoken with him. A friend had pointed him out to me. I believe my aunt assumed I knew the both of you because I knew of him. I was only in Harrington for such a short time. I do not believe he would recognize me or my name."

"Did you say you did not know us?" Brea asks, her voice rising.

"She assumed I knew of you."

"Nate has a very good memory," Stephen says in a soft, wary voice. "He may recognize you."

"I do not know if I would recognize him—I picture him as a twelve-year-old boy, young-looking for his age."

Brea winces.

Believing I should leave now—hasn't my time with them come to an end? Not wanting to go, I take a last sip of coffee and then stand up. I have come to Stephen and Brea because I am looking for something from them, something more than information about my aunt.

I move toward the door, recalling the harsh expression on Brea's face as she rebuffed the man I assume was her director that hot April afternoon, then abruptly kissing him on the mouth. And how I'd heard vaguely of Dr. Forester, never seeing him, or if I did, not knowing who he was—the husband of the actress from New York. He'd been ghost-like to me, not real.

Stephen, lightly tapping his foot on the floor, as if a melody is running through his head, grasps each hand onto an armrest. He rises from his chair to say good-bye. The word on his sweatshirt is now visible: "*Truth*?!!"

Early November. The curvy brim shields her eyes. She lifts her head, adjusts her hat, looks over at Nate. Asleep on the chaise lounge next to hers, Adrianna's gaze covers him. He's pushed his dark glasses atop his head, his hands lie evenly next to him, his expression is still; his almond-shaped lids, wide forehead are enhanced by the light.

Once he opens his eyes, she knows he will not appear intransigent as his current pose may suggest, but flexible, yielding, his arms extending as he speaks, his body agile, lanky. She is filled with a sense of futility and deep affection.

The heat from the sun pressing her head, she reclines against the matting of the chair. Nate insisted they take a Florida vacation before making a final decision about their future together. He had pleaded with her—he had never done so before. His insistence had surprised her—it wasn't in his nature, she had thought. And so she had relented.

He tends to put things off. She is convinced that one day when he has made a choice about his future, he will be the one to break off from her. If she had not left him that rainy night last May, he would not be trying to hold on to her—he doesn't want to experience the loss again. Her intuition tells her he is not in love with her. He confuses her, she thinks, closing her eyes.

What does she want? she asks. Truthfully? She doesn't know. If she did, she would not have agreed to come to Miami. Her uncertainty frustrates her more than his insistence.

She had gone to see him that day because she had needed to explain to him why she had left. Passion and fear are not logical or ethical, she acknowledges.

She has always leaned on her sense of fairness and logic; she needed to while growing up. Her parents had worked long hours in order to afford life in New York City.

Adrianna, the oldest of three children, needed to be the nanny. She would pick up her two younger brothers from school. Their teachers would often speak to Adrianna and not her parents about her siblings, who were six and seven years younger, respectively, than her. She was adept at listening and coherent in her response to the teachers' queries and suggestions. One of her brothers' teachers had said to her, "You understand your brother more than your mother does."

Adrianna had half-smiled—she knew it was true, but she

also admired her mother's career. A photographer, her mother traveled a lot and was quite focused on her work. Though she was intent as well as practical about her career, when it came to family matters and relationships, Adrianna's mother would allow her emotions to guide her. Tears would come to her eyes whenever a teacher questioned the behavior of one of her children—she took it personally—whereas her daughter did not take very much personally. Instead, she listened.

She turns her head again to Nate. His eyes are open.

"Nice of your parents to let us use their vacation week."

"Why wouldn't they?" he asks sleepily.

"Not everyone would."

"Let's go for a swim," he says. He stands up. His skin has a golden hue to it, sand clinging to his arms.

"I'll watch," she says; her smile is encouraging.

He looks back at her as he walks toward the shore. She is diverted by the sound of gulls, swooshing above.

Within minutes she sees him swimming in the ocean, his strokes steady, strong—and it strikes her that this may be who he is. Even-keeled. Determined. Closing her eyes, it strikes her that he isn't quite formed, that is why he does not love her. He cannot and may never be able to—he may remain in this adolescent stage forever. Despite the heat, she feels a chill and is discouraged.

Stepping out of the water, he comes towards her, his bathing trunks, soaking wet, wrapping his legs, a shadow briefly crossing him.

He drops himself onto the chaise lounge, his shoulders slouching. His head down, she sees sand on his feet and feels a pang for him, his vulnerability.

"Don't worry about me," he says.

"I am not worried about you—just uncertain."

"Uncertain?"

"About who you are."

Encouraged, he meets her gaze, "I am like you. We are different. We refuse to follow."

She feels herself tightening within.

"I don't know if what you say is true."

The sound of her voice, low and soft, pleases him. He looks out toward the horizon, a slight breeze ruffles his dark blond hair.

Overcome, she leans over, reaches out. With her fingers she searches his face—it is damp and warm from the sun. He squints. Taking off her hat, she gets out of her lounge chair. She lays beside him; she feels the wet of his bathing trunks against her bare legs and is comforted. They fall asleep in each other's arms.

We still do not know of Aunt Laura's whereabouts. My oldest brother, concerned about the stress of the situation on our mother, has asked a tall, heavy-set detective named Jimmy to look into it. After a few weeks, Jimmy informs us that he has no idea where she is. I wonder if he knows but is not saying, or he hasn't really looked for her. The detective speaks frankly, says she is an adult, she is able to make her own choices—her husband hasn't contacted the authorities. She has written a letter to her sister. He's concluded that she has left her husband voluntarily. She most likely is involved with another man. It is not unusual. It happens all the time. She is alive and apparently not under duress. What more do you expect?

A few weeks after the first letter, my mother receives another one from her sister—nothing in it suggests why she left her husband. All my aunt writes is, "You know I've always been a rebel at heart." The postmark again is indecipherable—she may be anywhere in the country.

My mother smiles ruefully and says, "I thought I was the spontaneous one."

My aunt's husband closed down their home and moved back to the West Coast, where he was born and lived until he was eighteen. I can imagine him, clean-shaven, packing up in his pointed and mildly distracted way—he always seemed to have other things on his mind despite his appearance as an orderly human being.

It appears that he has accepted her leaving him. At first I found this odd, but I have eventually come to understand it is because of the sort of relationship they have had. Though he may have been shaken at first, his sense of loss has not lasted very long. I try to convince myself it is because of the choices they have made and that neither of them are deeply upset by what has happened. Maybe they wanted their marriage to end in this way all along, maybe it is why they set it up as they had.

* * *

I have invited Craig to Thanksgiving dinner. His family is in Chicago. He was married once, for two years, is now divorced, and has no children. He does not open up very much about his relationship with his ex-wife. I do not want to pry; he might reveal something of himself that will disillusion me. I am not ready to give up—I tend to be a skeptic about most things; it is easy for me to be disappointed in a person. Yes, he is inscrutable. There is much to explore.

This Thanksgiving day my mother is circumspect; the trees are bare, skeletal shapes against a gray sky, and the air feels raw. We decide to go out to eat instead of having the holiday meal at her home. For some reason, she says, she doesn't possess the wherewithal to prepare a dinner. Half-heartedly, she greets Craig.

I know she is thinking of my father and realize this time of year may prompt some memory of him—whether good or bad, I am not certain.

My two brothers have come with their families; they arrived early this morning. They both live about an hour from my mother, though in opposite directions, one north of her and the other southwest.

Over dinner we discuss our aunt, not knowing where she is, and her husband's reaction, how upset he was at first and then how soon afterward he accepted her leaving him, almost easily and not grudgingly.

Craig appears keenly interested. I am not surprised. He has been with me from the start, the evening my aunt disappeared. It has been a focal point for us—there isn't a day we don't discuss her.

My aunt confuses me; she was there for me at a sensitive time in my life, and despite this, I understand I do not know her. She is a mystery—maybe she always was and I was too young to realize.

My mother looks searchingly around the table whenever she speaks of her sister, as if she believes one of us may know more about her whereabouts than she does. We remind her that she is the one her sister has written to, not any one of us.

When I look at my brothers, I am reminded of how in different ways they have been affected by our father's death. One brother, who used to be ebullient and happy, has turned out to be cautious and circumspect. I've seen photos of my father carrying him on his back, my brother's hands clenched tightly round our dad's neck. And my oldest brother was relaxed, an easygoing and affable adolescent, but has become a tense and nearly suspicious adult, rarely smiling.

I look over at Craig, wonder how he is experiencing my family. He listens but keeps his distance. I am uncertain about the two of us. Why do we keep seeing each other? We are different. He is more of an optimist than I am—sometimes I find his optimism overbearing, and I know he is uneasy at times with my doubting nature, but we can't separate. Is there more to why we are together than I realize—is there something I need to know? I look away from him, refusing to think deeply about him, or us.

To distract myself, I gaze over at my mother; she again is looking in a searching way around the table. It strikes me that she is not thinking one of us may know more about our aunt's whereabouts than she does. She is more aware than I have realized—she's debating whether or not to reveal to us the truth about her sister.

"What do you think?" He turns and looks over at Adrianna. She tilts her head to the right, assessing the Homer painting.

He and Adrianna have driven to Boston for the weekend to get away from New York, to begin Christmas shopping.

She isn't inclined to like scenic paintings—she finds most of them bleak. Portraits are more uplifting, she thinks. The two young boys in the center of the painting intrigue her. "It doesn't matter what I think—what do you think, Nate?" she asks. She takes a few steps closer to the work to view the boys.

He studies the painting for a few moments before answering. His voice low, he says, "I remember my parents discussing it when I was about the same age as those boys. My father liked it and my mother in her dramatic way said she found it boring, static. My father thought there was much stirring in the minds of the young boys—an early awareness, possibly, of their longings, their fears. He has always admired this work."

"Do you remember what you thought at the time?"

"No, I only remember the tension between my parents. The boys seem apprehensive. To me the painting resonates with tension, unease."

"And it still does?"

He shrugs. "Less so now." He turns to Adrianna and smiles. "Let's go—I'd like to walk some; it isn't too cold. And then I want to take you somewhere."

They walk up to Kenmore Square. Nate points to an older-style brick building with a curved windows, and says, "My grandfather's office was in there, not sure which floor. He was a controversial person—some people believed he was gifted and others thought he was a negative force. I guess it depended on your perspective—was he inventive and helpful, or ineffective and dark?"

"What do you think, Nate—or your father?"

"We don't talk of my grandfather."

"Then how do you know?"

"I've read news articles I found when we lived in Harrington, in a box beneath a pile of photos in my father's closet. I'd read them a few times each year, and the older I was, the more I understood. I have also spoken to my mother who really has no definite knowledge of my grandfather; she has only told me what she has pieced together. And then there is my mother's mother who has strong opinions, even now, in her nineties. Her opinions are firm, but she doesn't know of any facts either."

* * *

Soon they are driving north toward New Hampshire. "I want you to see where I grew up. Harrington is both a strange and picturesque town."

"You *are* a New Yorker."

"Yes, but Harrington is part of my life too. In fact, a woman from Harrington came to visit my parents three months ago. She needed to ask questions about her aunt who she thought had disappeared, but in fact it seems that she may have left her husband. This woman had lived with her aunt in Harrington for a few years, and thought my parents might know of her relative. She's from Massachusetts, close to Boston, and now lives in Connecticut. Harrington is not a mystery to all people, Adrianna."

She smiles. "Didn't you say your mother performed in the theater by the sea? I've heard of it."

He looks away from Adrianna, tightly clutches the steering wheel. The sky is gray and stark, only a few shades lighter than the road.

He's thinking of that morning in mid-August. He had spent the night at his friend's house; it would be the last time they'd be together before his buddy moved away. His friend had had his older brother buy beer for them to drink. Nate had been planning to spend the entire day with his friend, but had left his bathing suit in his bedroom. As he approached his home it seemed eerily quiet. He thought his father might have left for work already.

He realized he had forgotten his key and was worried his mother might not be there. He went up to the window at the front of the home. He peeked inside and saw his mother sprawled out on the couch, her head back against the sofa arm. Her director was kneeling close to her, running his fingers through her hair—she just lay there, did not respond. He felt queasy, his heart racing.

With abandon, he turned round and ran back to his friend's house, becoming sick along the way. He avoided directly looking at or speaking to his mother at any length for months. But once he went to boarding school the anger and pain had seemed to lessen.

As an adult he does not often recall that day—oftentimes he forgets, but mostly it is because he refuses to remember.

As they drive through the center of Harrington, Adrianna gazes out the window, notices a scattering of leafless trees, the small ones shaking from the wind. A variety of shops line the street. "Maybe we should have come during the spring or summer—it might be quaint and charming when it is sunny and warm," she says.

"We will take a quick look and then drive back to the hotel in Boston—we'll be there in time for dinner." He reaches for her hand.

She nods and looks straight ahead. He wonders if she is discouraged that he has taken her to Harrington on this gray and now cold day.

He first drives up to where his father's office was. When they get out of the car, a cold wind blows. Adrianna crosses her arms to keep herself warm. She shivers.

Nate points upward. "That is where his office was—I would wait in the outside area whenever I went to see him. I did not go very often."

Adrianna nods. Nate sees she is still shivering. "Let's get back in the car. I will show you where we lived and then I'll bring you to the theater where my mother performed."

He is disappointed. The town isn't exactly as he remembered. And Adrianna is only politely interested.

When they get back into the car, Adrianna bends forward to turn up the heat.

"On second thought, Adrianna, let's drive back to Boston now. It is too cold to be here today."

Touching his arm with her gloved hand, Adrianna says, "It's okay, Nate."

"I don't know if I want to come here again. It is not real to me." He feels a deep sense of loss, wanting to hold on to what was, and is deeply aware that not only does it no longer exist, it never will again. He is reaching for memories, but they have flattened out—have deflated—and probably will never inflate again or, if so, not as they were, but in a more illusory form.

As he puts the car in gear, he recalls riding on the scooter next to his friend on those long summer days, the sense of endless freedom, and how when his buddy left Harrington, Nate had no one else to fill the hole of that lost friendship. A year later, he was no longer in touch with his friend and on occasion would wonder if their relationship had been as idyllic as he remembered, and then afterward, it was as if it had never been.

While he attended boarding school in Boston, his parents would visit him nearly every weekend, take him out to dinner, to a play or movie, or to listen to music in an old church in Copley Square. And then there were certain winter months when his mother would perform at a theater in the city, and so she was nearby and would stop by and see him every evening before she went in to the theater. At the school, he developed friendships with a number of boys his age. Though Boston was more subdued than New York, he was relieved to be in a city again.

He looks over at Adrianna, studies her profile. He always thinks of her as facing him—she'll turn to him when they are together. It is who she is—never hiding anything, always hoping to be straightforward. Then he thinks of the night she left him, and is still bothered by it. His gaze falls on her slanting cheekbone, the upturned nose, the narrow chin, and full lips. He anticipates that one day she will leave him again, but he is not ready for them to separate. He will do anything to prevent that feeling of loss. Though it only was for two days, it was a painful forty-eight hours. He is not ready to experience it again. He's never thought of himself as weak, but he feels he is when it comes to Adrianna.

He imagines her as a young girl, taking care of her two young brothers, her expression determined. While making dinner for the family, she'd instruct them to do their homework at the kitchen table. She'd take glimpses out the window to view the city, half-smiling, longing to know her future, envisioning herself performing at Carnegie Hall.

* * *

As they are about to cross the border into Massachusetts, there is a blockage at the tolls. They are stuck in traffic. Nate puts on the radio to see if there is any news about the delay. But there is no mention of a problem at the border.

There are many police cars and a few ambulances.

Nate turns to Adrianna, "Drug bust?"

She shrugs, and looks down at her phone, "I will check to see if there is anything I can find online."

"Look," Nate calls out; Adrianna raises her face.

They see a covered body on a stretcher being lifted onto an ambulance.

Then Adrianna notices a woman being led away by police.

"It's a woman," she says.

"Can't tell if she is in handcuffs," he responds, craning his neck.

"She's in her fifties, I think. Looks harmless—devastated. I imagine her life will never again be the same."

I learn of my aunt's arrest a few weeks after it occurred. Craig and I were traveling, and my mother did not want to interrupt our vacation. She was happy I was involved in a relationship with a decent person. Before we left for our trip to London, she had said, pointing her forefinger straight ahead, her eyes narrowing, that she wanted me to enjoy myself as much as possible. By referring to him as "decent," I knew she liked Craig, but was hesitant in saying more, believing she had misjudged my relationships in the past. She is much quieter than she was ten years ago, much more cautious and questioning—she's lost her spontaneity, it seems. I cannot decide which version of my mother I prefer, or if there is a third one about to be revealed.

We return from our trip a week before Christmas. More hopeful than I've ever been. My relationship with Craig is fulfilling, and yet I have no expectations. I enjoy living in southern Connecticut, appreciate going into New York for a day whenever I choose to do so.

Over the phone, her voice resigned, my mother informs me of her sister's arrest.

"There must be some sort of mistake," I say, my heart pounding. Aunt Laura arrested, I repeat to myself again and again.

She tells me that through a friend of a friend she has found her sister a strong lawyer. She is weary from relaying news that is not uplifting, that she knows has startled me.

She is unable to give me the exact details but it has to do with the man my aunt was involved with—he was shot and killed while trying to escape. My aunt had been with him in his van when police cars began to follow them. Suddenly, her lover slammed on the brakes, then dropped out of the van, leaving the door open, and ran into the woods. My aunt was in the passenger seat.

The detectives want to know if my Aunt Laura has had any involvement in his activities or if she is an innocent friend or lover. That is all my mother knows. She does not sound upset, and I understand it to mean she is relieved her sister has been located.

Memories of my aunt fill my mind, how she would take me shopping, stand close to me, surveying what was before us. She instilled in me a sense of calm, a sense of detachment. She and her husband did not communicate very much; the silence surrounding the dinner table was settling and painful. And then the last time I visited her—wasn't she expecting someone? And how she had mentioned the Forester family. Had they been a red herring to divert me from asking other questions? Questions about the nearly two years I stayed with her and her husband in Harrington? Had I missed something when I lived with them? All those hours I was left alone. I am not certain if my memories of that time are real or ones I have created to comfort myself.

"I need to see her," I say.

III

Adrianna

That summer day in the small cramped grocery store, wearing our covid masks, we, at first, did not realize we had met briefly in Rome the year before. Later Nate would tell me that though the market was just around the corner from his apartment building, he had shopped there only on occasion. And so he was convinced our second meeting had been fate. I answered that I often had gone into the grocery store—I wasn't certain you would call it fate, but it was a chance meeting.

We had been standing near each other in the crowded checkout aisle, closer than most would during that time. Customers were not adhering to the separation requirements while in line—the store was too small.

We sensed that we'd seen each other before, but were not

certain. Whenever I moved slightly forward, the small basket I carried, filled with berries, cheese, and crackers, skimmed his back but he did not turn round or flinch. I could hear his breaths—short and sharp. Eight or so people were waiting in line before us. I was uncomfortable; it was a steamy early August day. I felt as if I were suffocating, my throat dry, my face covering oppressive. He didn't seem bothered by his mask, did not appear uneasy as many did at that time—this odd situation we were all in then. I gleaned it could have been any day for him—it wasn't as if we were in the middle of a pandemic. I thought he might be one of these people who, so focused on the details of his life, was immune to what was going on around him, unaffected by it, or, on the other hand, was unaware and distant, completely wrapped up in himself. He piqued my curiosity. I attributed it to the haze of familiarity that sometimes is real and at other times could be a trick of memory.

I had been very affected by the isolation—I had never been circumspect until those years. I'd always been more forward-thinking.

As I paid for my groceries, I noticed him dawdling near the exit area. I was surprised. Passing him on my way out, I heard a muffled "hi." It was so faint I wasn't certain it was coming from him. When I looked up, I met his gaze, felt myself grinning beneath my mask. His eyes were an unusual blend of green and brown.

I think if it had not been during the pandemic, we would not have been hesitant. Although it was not very long ago, it was a different time then. Most of us were not free, and that was what intrigued me about Nate; the more I got to know him, the more I was aware that he was not burdened by the restrictions placed upon us. It seemed as if he rose above them, while the rest of us, to a lesser or greater degree, cowered. And I cowered too, but in the group that did so to a lesser degree. Though, yes, it was cowering.

That summer day we made our way to a coffee shop a few blocks away. We sat outside and were allowed to lower our masks to drink or to eat. The moment before we dropped our face coverings was very intense; each of us was outwardly uncomfortable. I don't know who lowered the mask first, or maybe we did so simultaneously. At that moment we knew for certain we had met in Rome the previous summer, at the bottom of the Spanish Steps. We both laughed, and a balmy breeze, lingering before dissolving, relaxed us even more.

What was it that drew me to Nate that day? It was more than a vague sense of him seeming as if he were someone I might know—he stirred something within me, his inquisitive expression, honest, direct.

Later he said he was curious to see what the rest of my face looked like—he had been struck with how familiar my eyes had seemed, dark and warm, that he might have looked into them once.

I then asked if he had been surprised by my appearance. I had changed my hairstyle since he had last seen me. He shook his head as if he had already gone on to other thoughts, that my full appearance was what he expected—everything matched as it had when we had first seen each other in Italy.

* * *

We did not truly become a couple until a year after our second meeting. Over the time we've been together, my intention has been to be honest with him and fair—it has always been a priority of mine in any relationship.

My conclusion about him is that yes, to an extent, he is in touch with his emotions, yet he is distant from them at the same time. It is his distance that prevents me from expressing what I need to say. Though, at times, he seems innocent, not necessarily naive, more unsuspecting.

From the beginning he has trusted me and because of this I have remained silent, and at times evasive with him. His innocence, his sense of trust, has become a burden for me. He doesn't understand why I left him without an explanation that night. But my sense of fairness did prevail. A few days later, going back to the bookstore on Broadway, where I assumed he would be, his expression relaxed when he noticed me. I gathered that on one level he was expecting me and on another he thought I would never return to him.

* * *

About nine months after meeting Nate in front of the Spanish Steps, I was with my grandmother in Central Park—it was in the early days of the pandemic, May, I believe. My grandmother is quite beautiful, despite her age, and that was what I was thinking of that day in Central Park. She had been telling me how she was longing to return to Europe again once this wretched virus had passed. Then she suddenly stopped talking. I believe Nate at that point was walking by with his mother—though I never saw him that day. They had passed us before I realized my grandmother was pointing them out.

"There is the stage actress Brea and I think she may be with her son." I turned my head in the direction she was indicating and caught a glimpse of Brea but did not see her son. Brea wore large dark glasses and it was difficult to notice any individual feature about her. And then she disappeared into a crowd of people.

"I've never heard of Brea, I mean an actress with a first name only," I answered, "and I did not really see her—I would not recognize her if she passed us again." As I was about to ask how she knew of Brea, I remembered that my grandmother was a great admirer of off-Broadway productions and would often drive from her home in Boston to New York to see a play.

Over the years my grandmother and I have grown close; I am the one she has confided in. I have always been a good listener and she has liked to talk, though she has told me that most of her life she has been secretive and it has not served her well. "Adrianna, honesty is more important than silence. I used to think otherwise. I was mistaken."

I listened to her, convinced that I was not secretive as my grandmother had been. It is why I returned to Nate.

Early on, I understood that Nate knew how to cope in a natural way with restrictions, that he was unflappable in the face of them—maybe to an extent he was freed by rules. This is what compelled me to know him. For I, on the other hand, was oppressed by the limitations placed upon us, and felt horribly confined; it was why I had been drawn to Nate. I needed to learn how to be free when our society no longer was.

Lainie

Aunt Laura was not detained long by the police. She was put under house arrest for a few months—the authorities wanted to be certain everything checked out before clearing her, that she was as innocent as they had assumed. No one believed she was without blame. Is it not more appropriate to ask whether or not she was culpable? She must have had some inkling that her "boyfriend's" behavior had aroused her suspicions. She pointedly claimed she had no idea that he was selling drugs or had guns in his possession. If he didn't have a job, how could he afford his lifestyle? Had she never asked those questions of him or to herself? There was no apparent evidence against her, and still they needed more time before completely freeing her.

* * *

Rebecca, my mother, and my aunt Laura were the only two siblings in their family. They were raised in a suburb of Boston, not far from where I grew up. It was a mixture of people of different backgrounds. My mother was older than her sister, but they were only a little over a year apart.

My grandmother had married at a later age, two years short of forty. My mother was born when she was thirty-nine and a few months, and my grandmother was over forty when she gave birth to my aunt. Like the community they lived in, my family was mixed as well—my grandmother had attended college and one year of law school. She didn't complete her law degree because she realized it wasn't practical enough for her. Because of her mathematical skills, she reached a high position in a research company at a time when computers were beginning to become recognized as integral to our society. She was employed until she married my grandfather, who was an electrician, much older than herself and nearing retirement. His first marriage had ended in divorce. He'd been quite young and his wife had left him for another man early on. It had taken him years to trust a woman again. He appreciated my grandmother's sharp intelligence and was not intimidated by it. I never met him but heard he was very kind, whereas my grandmother may have been too practical, and not very maternal. My mother would say, pointing her finger upward, that her mother was an optimist. I was uncertain of what my aunt thought of my grandmother as she rarely spoke of her feelings or preferences.

My mother and Aunt Laura had different strengths and so there was little competition between the two sisters. My grandmother was widowed when she was forty-eight, before either my mother or aunt were ten, and so my mother and aunt had come to maturity with no father present.

Of the two sisters, my mother was more quiet in front of relatives and friends—though she was older, she was smaller than her sister, bosomy, narrow shoulders and hips. My aunt was a little above average in height with a medium bone structure. Though my mother was shy in front of strangers, she was more emotional with her parents and her sister, readily expressing her feelings. Her mother and father, having been older and more stoic, though in different ways, were often confused by my mother, I have gathered.

Aunt Laura appeared more measured and thoughtful, not as sensitive or as intuitive as my mother. My grandparents must have felt more comfortable with my aunt and because of it I assume they gave her more freedom. She appeared more responsible than my mother. Since the two sisters were opposite from one another, each accepted her sibling. They followed their individual interests—my mother was poetically inclined and Aunt Laura was interested in sociology. Social justice.

My mother attended college in the city, not too far from their home. She met my father at a poetry reading. He was in attendance not because he enjoyed poetry but because if he went to a few readings he would be exempted from writing a paper for a required English class. He had hoped to become an engineer. But my parents were a passionate couple. They married soon afterward, my oldest brother born six months later.

* * *

As Aunt Laura's husband had filed for divorce and shut down the house, readying it for sale, she needed to find an apartment in Harrington; she knew the town well and could not leave the state at this time.

For a variety of reasons—my work, my travels from Connecticut to Massachusetts, and my mother's strong suggestion that she needed to see her sister first and alone to determine what had happened—it was three months before I visited Aunt Laura.

My mother called me after meeting with her sister; she was satisfied with how her sister was coping, though she didn't give any specific details why this was so.

My understanding is that my mother now believes this episode with her sister is over. She is free again to resume her life—my mother is dating for the first time and appears confident. The last time she appeared content was when my father was alive.

Until recently, I did not know that after my father's passing and the mourning period that followed, my mother became aware of my aunt and uncle's lifestyle, how vague and insubstantial it was. It was why I returned home to Massachusetts earlier than expected.

It would have been difficult for Aunt Laura and her husband to give my mother the support she might need after my father died. So steeped in the pain she was experiencing from her husband's passing and because of the fog she was in, my mother was at first oblivious to her sister and brother-in-law's behavior. I do not think she would have sent me to live with them if she had known; once she became aware, she immediately extracted me from the situation.

* * *

On this early spring day, the wind is sharp and the sun strong, I press the bell outside Aunt Laura's apartment building. It is a medium-sized structure with a white concrete exterior. Waiting for her to buzz me in, my apprehension grows. Once I am inside, I slowly climb the two flights to the floor where she lives.

She opens the door, and I am struck by the lack of expression on her face, how much weight she has lost, how she does not meet my gaze. She doesn't smile initially and when she does, it is with effort. She has gone through so much since I saw her eight months ago. I have a list of questions in mind, but once I see her I realize she may not be capable of answering any one of them.

She ushers me inside her apartment. It looks stark, the furniture is made of an inexpensive teak. A sofa sits in the corner of the room, a chair has been placed across from it, both perpendicular to a large vacant window. A simple and small coffee table stands between the sofa and chair. There is an empty glass vase on the table, a plain rectangular shape. She motions for me to sit on the sofa and she sits in the small chair. She rests her hand lightly on the narrow armrest and looks toward me with a touch of her old confidence, the expression on her face takes on its old solidity, and she raises her chin slightly as she did in the past, as we were about to leave her home, on our way out to do errands. Her manner always provided me with an assurance I'd not experienced before.

Yet today is different; she is unable to maintain her air of confidence. My heart beats quickly, softly—there is so much I need to ask, but I realize on this first visit it is best for me to listen to her, her story. She looks steadily at me, and in a quiet voice, she says, "Lainie."

My hands clasped on my lap, I wait for her to say more. Strong early spring light brightens the apartment, a ray crossing her face soon disappears.

"Lainie," she says again. "There is so much to say, and I do not know if I am capable enough to explain or if I understand enough to do so."

I remain silent, concerned that if I speak, I will disrupt her reflective mood. I long to hear her words. She gets up from her chair comes over to me, lowers her head and with her forefinger, she touches my scar. Uncertain, I sit up erectly, not knowing what she will do or say next.

"Do you remember?" she speaks softly,

I part my lips but do not respond.

"Don't you remember?"

I shake my head, not knowing what she is referring to.

"That day when you were five, we came to visit you in Massachusetts."

I shake my head again. She leaves me and goes over to the window, stands with her back to me. "Oh, come now, Lainie, you *must* remember." I hear the old determination in her voice and feel hopeful.

"It was summer, and your mother and father—it was their anniversary, your mother was wearing a medium-blue colored dress, an A-line shape; she looked more beautiful than I'd ever seen her. We had come to watch you and your brothers, but we came mostly for you because you were the youngest and needed the most care. Your brothers could very well have gone to a friend's home for a sleepover." She crosses her arms and turns round to face me.

I half-smile at her and shrug, my hands still on my lap. She starts to come toward me again, but stops and decides instead to sit again in the narrow chair. She grips her hands on the edges of her seat, her expression wistful, her tone nearly harsh. "You *don't* recall?" she asks, as if reprimanding me.

I shrug again and say, "I was young then, Aunt Laura—I do not remember much of that time, especially since my father passed; those years are a blur to me. Even if I hadn't lost my father at thirteen, I do not think most children recall much of what happened when they were five—maybe a quick memory without any context." While I speak, I feel a sense of the unknown, as if I am entering a completely dark room in a hotel I've not been to before and I am groping for a light switch.

She seems to relax a bit when I say this, her hands no longer tightly holding on to the edges of her chair.

"Do you remember our visiting you?" I close my eyes and try to bring an image to mind. I hear her words now sounding soft and vague with a hint of desperation, "Try Lainie, try to remember, try for *my* sake."

After a few moments, I say to her, my eyes still closed, "I cannot force myself to recall, Aunt Laura. I have never liked to dwell on the past or pull up memories. Maybe I have been too practical to do so. I've needed to look ahead and not behind. I don't believe memories are reliable, factual."

"I envy you, Lainie," she says, an undercurrent of emotion in her voice I've not heard from her before. "When I was your age, I thought the same."

Carefully, she rises from her seat. She walks over to me again, her face and shoulders tilting to the side. Standing before me, her expression is expectant, yet unknowing, like a child uncertain whether or not they have done anything wrong.

Leaning forward, she strokes my scar with her forefinger and says in a whisper, "It is me, because of me."

I remain still, thinking how much I had admired her.

Laura

Gently I embrace my niece, press her close to me. Then I step away, and for the third time this day I touch her scar, believing it is mine.

I watch her walk down the corridor, her shoulders erect; no longer does she appear slim and lithe, but strict and tense. Before she reaches the elevator, she turns and waves good-bye, her lips tight with disappointment.

I understand I will not see her again for a while. Her mother, my sister, will be my guardian, so to speak. She always knew my potential for extreme behavior, though few others would have guessed. Yet despite her knowledge of me, she has told me she cannot comprehend why I became involved with a dark and destructive person—I who'd always been an advocate for social justice, for fairness, kindness to all.

Neither my sister nor Lainie understand that he was not criminal to me; he was warm and imperfect, never abusive. Had he ever revealed any violent inclinations? If he had, had I been blind to them? Of course, I had suspicions, but only suspicions, and in the past I'd had many suspicions about people that I discovered were not true. He had moved me, shaken my sense of objectivity, my calculations about life and people. I was a different person with him, free, loving. Not only had I not been this way before, I had thought I was incapable of passion, of giving myself unconditionally to another person.

Closing the door to my apartment, I lock it carefully, and it strikes me that Lainie may very well have left more confused than when she first came this afternoon. I had explained to Lainie that when she was five, and we'd been babysitting her, she had been sitting next to me. My husband at the time had left the room. Suddenly she had grasped my hand and snatched the cigarette I was smoking. I watched as she held it between her fingers, bringing it to her lips, mirroring me. I was calm and allowed her to do so, believing I was in control of the situation. I let her hold the cigarette for too long. I had been intrigued by her desire to imitate me. She ran the ember of the cigarette down the side of her face. Her expression stoic as she ran the burning cigarette up and down her face, immune to the pain. I had watched her, had not stopped her. When my husband came into the room and realized what was happening, he picked her up, and took the cigarette from her.

As I spoke of this to Lainie today, she remained impassive, didn't move from her seat. I could not fathom what was going through her mind.

Lainie is fond of me, appreciates that I was there for her after her father died, but she does not fully understand who I am. The only question she asked me, just before she left, was why I had mentioned the Forester family last July. But she did not wait for my answer. Instead she said that she thought the son had seemed alone, and observing him had helped her realize that she was alone too—they were two lonely children, staring at each other from a distance. Shrugging, she then got up to leave.

I have given so much up for my passion—my marriage, my relationship with my niece who I am fond of. I am left with nothing. I wonder if my love for him was an illusion instead of as real and visceral as I believed it to be.

I go over to the window, hoping to catch a glimpse of Lainie driving away. But there is no trace of her—she must have parked on the other side of the building. I feel a rushing and harsh sense of pain. I bang on the glass with my fists, then retreat to my chair to calm myself.

Brea

Although I had needed to, I'd never really liked Harrington. I found it not quaint but placid, intellectualized, simplistically so. Passionless. Because of my desire to move away from New York at the time, I ignored my initial impressions and plunged forward, agreeing to live there.

On our first visit, I forced myself to imagine how lovely it would be—a peaceful environment for our young son; he'd have space to run about. I remember standing outside the theater for the first time, wanting to believe it was perfect. I took a deep breath of sea air and was momentarily elated. But I knew I was deluding myself. Yet, as I have said, I needed to like Harrington.

Stephen and I had decided to leave New York because we both understood it was time to make a change. Our apartment was too small for the three of us. Stephen was tired from his many hours of hospital work, and I was not getting the opportunity to play the roles I wanted to. I knew if I didn't look for a theatrical experience that would allow me to perform parts that were in line with my classical training, I might never have the chance to do so. Procuring a lead role in New York theater was challenging, and I enjoyed the intensity of it until I realized time was passing and I might not ever be given a preferred part in a play by Chekhov or Ibsen. And so for the three of us, for different reasons, we realized it was imperative for us to leave New York.

I was aware that Harrington was not and would never be a place for me. Though I believed it would be easier for Stephen to adapt to a small New Hampshire city than myself, I doubted it would be the ideal place for him, but assumed it would be good enough. And when the tragedy of September 11th occurred a year after we left the city, we began to accept that moving away from New York had been the right choice after all.

That year I attempted to become interested in what was going on in the town. I began to converse with people while shopping or in line at a movie theater. At first those I spoke with were not very different from the people we knew in New York—they shared the same political leanings, and were interested in the arts, though not necessarily passionate about them. They enjoyed attending sporting events, and depending on the season would spend weekends cross-country skiing or hiking, preferring the natural world, which Stephen and I had never been inclined to appreciate.

We had been immersed in city life during our years in New York—the theater, art museums, opera, book readings. The people we met in Harrington helped us realize there was more to life than the proclivities of many New Yorkers. Yet even though we attempted to be open, tried hiking and cross-country skiing, because of who we were and where we had come from, we could never really adjust to Harrington life.

It took another year to acknowledge to myself and to Stephen that there was much more going on below the surface of this town and it was then that I became uneasy, mildly insecure. Slowly, I was becoming enamored with my director—he made me feel attractive and I erroneously believed he protected me from the pettiness of small town life. I suppressed my interest in him for quite a few years, that was, until I no longer could.

If I had acknowledged my feelings about Harrington from the start, maybe things would have been different. It was the smallness of the town in terms of size, not the small-mindedness of its people, that led me astray. For I learned that a small town can turn the minds of its residents small, even if they were not that way originally—it sort of creeps up on you. It creeps up on different people in different ways, as it did for me and Stephen.

About the same time, Stephen became overly preoccupied with his work—I had not seen him uninterested in our son or our marriage before. Uninterested may be the wrong word; maybe it is better to say not as focused as he had always been. In the past he enjoyed hearing about our son's day-to-day activities and had always enjoyed inquiring about a role I was playing, how I would approach it, and so on. But at one point, even though he asked the same questions he always had about our son and my work, he seemed no longer intrigued. I assumed it might have to do with his work and so I did not pry and just went along with my life.

I am not proud of my affair with Sam—it was short-lived, but intense. Anger was stirring within me. Why were we there? Whatever made us think we could live in Harrington? I was resentful we had moved there—yet I was as responsible as Stephen was for doing so. My excitement about playing different roles was frustrated by the indifference of the other actors I worked with. It wasn't that they didn't have ability; they were not as committed as I was to the theater. It had taken me a few years to realize this. I had never been attracted to Sam—my growing passion for him was unexpected.

Following the summer of my affair, Stephen and I acknowledged to each other what had happened and took steps to make things better for us and for our son. Stephen told me he had been preoccupied with a patient who had come to see him and who had seen his father years before, it had brought up old memories, painful ones, and so he had become more distracted than he usually was with his work. That was all he could tell me. He referred this patient—I am not certain if it was a man or woman—to another doctor.

After a year or so of trying to make things somewhat better, we saw that our son needed to get away more than we did and so for high school we sent him to a boarding school in Boston. I no longer performed in the Harrington theater. Instead I mostly took on roles in Boston, which was only about an hour or so from our home. I would get to see our son whenever I performed in the city. Stephen and I were dutiful about visiting him on weekends.

When the young woman, Lainie, came to our apartment in New York, we were uneasy. Though Stephen and I attempted to be welcoming, her presence brought us back to those years of living in Harrington. We were concerned she might have information that we were not aware of, perhaps of an incident in Harrington, and that because of our preoccupations, we had been oblivious to it, and might or might not have been connected to it in some way.

When it comes to Harrington, Stephen and I feel a tremendous amount of guilt. While there, we were not our best selves.

Stephen

When Lainie Moreau first contacted us, I suspected there was more to her story, more than she presented. Meeting and speaking with her a few days later, I understood she was honest and unaware of the complexity of the situation; there were more layers to it than she could possibly realize. And she appeared to be a factual person, not one to spend much time pondering. She was composed, her eyes observant, dispassionate.

We wanted to be helpful, but neither Brea nor I had been comfortable living in Harrington, and any mention of the small New Hampshire city could be jarring, like bumping into an ex-friend with whom you had had a discomforting relationship.

Throughout our years there, I accepted the people of Harrington for who they were—most were thoughtful, practical. I could tolerate our life not only because of my work—my practice was quite full and time-consuming—but because of my profession. Physicians need to accept first in order to hopefully heal.

Brea's desire was to appreciate Harrington, become part of the theatrical community, but she soon became impatient with her colleagues. Though she was able to take on roles she had longed to play—Shakespeare's Cleopatra, Ibsen's Mrs. Alving, and others—she grew disillusioned with the other actors, their lack of commitment to the art of performance as well as their indifference to interpreting with any depth the characters they played. This, of course, was her opinion.

I admire no one as much as I do Brea. I recall her walking out of the theater in New York the night we first met, her quick step, her ready smile. I had just seen her perform the role of Gwendolen in *The Importance of Being Earnest.* She was a brilliant comedic actress, I had believed. I think of that evening whenever I am disappointed in her, in us, in myself.

Once we realized small-town life was not good for our son Nate, we sent him to a boarding school in Boston. It was at this point that we began to organize our exit from Harrington and our eventual return to New York where we belong.

Through my work in Harrington I had come in contact with many people—it was the type of small city where people knew much about one another, especially those who had lived there for some time. And so private information about others was discussed during sessions with me.

When Lainie told us of her aunt, I assumed that I must have heard of her at some point during my time practicing in Harrington. Though I do not believe I had met her, her name was vaguely familiar, so much so that I could have heard of it from any person.

The uneasiness I first experienced in Lainie's presence was because I was attempting to remember and was frustrated that I was not able to do so. Even if I had been able to recall the name from my time practicing in Harrington, I would not have been able to relay information to Lainie for reasons of privacy.

After Lainie' second visit, the patient who had told me of Lainie's aunt contacted me. She left a voice message saying that her present psychiatrist was retiring and she was looking for a referral. I read my notes on this patient and came across the name, Laura Ringel, Lainie's aunt.

Our sessions had been pretty intense and my patient spoke of very little other than the issues most pressing to her. Yet, according to my notes, there was one occasion when she mentioned Lainie's aunt. She had met her in Harrington, and had discovered they were from the same city in Massachusetts. Because of this my patient was concerned this woman might have heard unfortunate information about her family of origin.

My patient remarked on this woman's marriage, it was an unusual marriage—one she could not understand. Although my patient had been married twice, she could not comprehend how her friend could lead a life like that. Why not simply leave him if you are unhappy? she had asked. The woman had responded that she was not unhappy—that it was a good lifestyle for her and her husband as they were both rebels. And that going against the grain was what contented and bonded them. My husband and I do not believe in living a balanced life, she had added, it is too traditional a concept for us. My patient could not relate to this woman—she thought she had created herself, her persona, that her words were not authentic.

I had written an extensive note of this session because I was pleased and encouraged by my patient's reaction to this woman—I believed she was making progress, the therapy was working.

My patient did not mention Laura Ringel again, and naturally I forgot about her. Though when Lainie came and told her story, there was something familiar about it. Because I did not recognize the name of Lainie's aunt as a former patient, I had assumed one of my Harrington clients may have mentioned her to me.

When I checked the date of my note, I realized the session occurred during the summer our life began to change. It was a time of strain for both Brea and me.

Brea's affair with Sam Wilkins was her means of acting out the stress in our relationship. I considered it my fault as much as hers. I had been absent emotionally from her that summer, intoxicated not with a particular patient, but with my own childhood. In the past I had not been inclined to think much of my youth, but that summer I could not prevent myself from doing so.

I eventually referred this patient who had spoken of Lainie's aunt to another psychiatrist. My former patient may have seen the truth about Lainie's aunt when others hadn't. She was perceptive. She had lived in Harrington only for a short while. She later wrote to me to say she was pleased with the person I had referred her to.

And now she is calling again because her doctor is retiring; he is in his eighties and not well. She asked, at the end of her voice message, if it would be possible for me to see her again.

IV

Nate peers out the front window of his parents' apartment; it is a gray Saturday afternoon, early April. He sees a line-up of cars with lights on. Squinting, he is able to make out a thin rain. He is alone now. Both Adrianna and his parents are away.

Adrianna is traveling in Europe—her grandmother invited her. Her grandfather had decided not to go at the last minute. He'd been gifted prime tickets to a basketball game and would not be able to use them if he traveled to Europe. Adrianna and her grandmother will be away for ten days, while his mother and father are spending two weeks in California: one week in the desert, and the next, a drive up the coast.

He did not expect to be invited on the trip with Adrianna, and he believes it is best for his parents to have time away from him, their concerns about him hovering over them whenever he is in their presence. Their half-worries are for reasons he does not want to consider; easily he shrugs them off. He is adept rather than stern in his refusal to bend to the will of others; his sense of autonomy is of foremost importance to him—it keeps him balanced, unencumbered.

He does not particularly like this time of year—almost warm and sunny at one moment, cold and windy at the next. Though he likes the light—it is what is best about early April—it takes away a sense that things seem hidden; now everything is visible. Light is revealing, not secretive.

When his parents are away, he'll often stay in their apartment. He connects with them more when they are absent. The hush of their non-presence lends him a sense of solace. For whenever he is with them, he sees an uneasiness between them. Though when he is in their living space and they are not, there is a lingering warmth, a subtle sense of harmony in their home. When he is not present they must be more relaxed, content to be in each other's company. This pleases him. Though he will always be uncertain about their relationship.

He misses Adrianna's energetic presence—but doesn't miss her constant questioning of their relationship her inability to accept what is before her. Why can't she accept things as they are? He feels a deep frustration. It is momentary. He recalls what he relishes about her, her sensitivity to her surroundings, her natural understanding of people, her quiet sense of humor.

Turning away from the window, he is struck with how

alone he is. Is he alone in knowledge—might there be information that he lacks that others are aware of? Is he missing Adrianna more than he could have imagined? Unlike his mother and father, Adrianna's absence does not evoke another dimension of her; it is as if she has vanished to another part of the world. His apartment feels empty, no trace of Adrianna's presence or lack of it.

He thinks of the evening before she left—they were coming in after a late dinner in Midtown, and she had gone from room to room switching on all the lights in his apartment, sighing, looking about, as if she wanted to remember every aspect of the place. Did she want to recall it while she was away? She had hardly looked at him, concentrating more on his place.

He now goes into his father's small study, just off the kitchen. It is very narrow, only enough room for a desk and a chair. Nate likes the view from the one window above the desk, a three-dimensional view of the Museum of Modern Art, which invariably uplifts him. He thinks of Van Gogh's *The Starry Night* in the museum—though he is not drawn to Van Gogh's works, he finds this painting energizing. Before he looks through the glass, he notices that his father has printed out an email and has placed it over the keyboard. Maybe he planned to take it with him on the trip? Nate glances down; by his father's guarded tone in the first few lines, he knows he is concerned about whomever he is writing to. There is no mention of a name and the email address has been blacked out. He picks it up and continues to read.

I received your voice message. Thank you for including your email address. It is good to know you are doing well, though I am sorry to hear of Dr. B.'s illness. It must be disappointing to you he will no longer be practicing. Yet I imagine you are pleased that your sessions with him these past fourteen years were of deep value to you, as you have mentioned.

When you revealed to me that my father had been your psychiatrist and had used unorthodox methods in treating you, which may very well have crossed a legal line, and that he also had had an extramarital relationship with your aunt, your guardian at the time, I realized I could not accept you as a patient.

You have done a lot of good work with Dr. B.—it is time for you to move forward and extricate yourself from the past. Even if it were ethical for me to take you on as a patient, I would only be a reminder to you of what you have already superseded. I am pleased to know your life has been a success since our last session, and that you continue to keep a journal. I am confident Dr. B. will refer you to a good doctor.

Best wishes,

Stephen Forester, M.D.

Nate recalls the newspaper clippings at the bottom of the box of photographs—what had been said about his grandfather. There never had been any legal renderings. But he was not a good man. Destructive? Evil? Will he ever know?

A sharp buzz brings Nate to the present. He goes to the door, doesn't speak into the intercom or ask for a name, just reflexively presses the button to let whoever it is in.

Tuesday, April 1: Rain this morning is intermittent. Craig's flight to Chicago leaves at 5:30 AM. I drive him to the airport. Both of us are silent, still not fully awake. Before stepping out of the car, he turns to me. Keep me informed, he says, his hand over mine. Then he smiles sheepishly, embarrassed by how solemn he sounds.

As I make my way through the traffic, I decide I'll write down a few notes each day so that when he returns in ten days, I'll be able to recap to him what has been happening without trying to recall and missing something in the process. When we talk at night, I want our conversation to be upbeat, not filled with extraneous details. If anything comes up, I will wait until he returns so we can speak face-to-face, in person. Invariably he asks questions, many questions. He should have been a lawyer or a detective. He will be visiting family, but I believe he will see his ex-wife. I asked him two days ago, and he said it wasn't on his schedule to do so, then he looked away as any honest person would do. And I assumed, hearing he was coming, she may have contacted him, wanting to see him. She is the party who ended the marriage, and those are usually the ones who want to return to it, realizing they didn't appreciate the other person enough during their time together.

* * *

Thursday, April 3: Slightly dispirited, I make dinner. Work was not productive today. I held a meeting and no one was really listening—twenty minutes into it, two co-workers began arguing, disagreeing on a matter that had nothing to do with why I had called everyone together. I tried to reason with them, but neither of them heard me. Since Craig has been away, no one seems to be listening anymore. They all know we are involved and because he is not here, it seems as if they don't take me seriously. It is as if I am only half-present. Never experienced this before. I will let Craig know once he returns—it is not something to bring up over the phone, or through FaceTime.

Since he left two days ago, I have been thinking about my time in Harrington. Last night I had a dream—a hazy one that I only vaguely recalled when I awoke. It was and wasn't like Harrington—the grayish sky, the uneven landscape, winding streets—El Greco's *View of Toledo* comes to mind. Though many like this work, I have felt uneasy looking at it—it is as if the viewer is looking into the inner workings of a manipulative person's thoughts.

In the dream I was confused with who was and wasn't trustworthy—many people were passing by, some stopping to converse. It was the same dark landscape and haunting imagery of El Greco's painting, but with figures. I can't recall a face other than in a vague way, slipping away from me before I understood who the person really was, pedestrians were partially shielded by veils or hoods. And I am left with that feeling of uncertainty—it is what prevailed once I awoke. The strong feeling of uncertainty is distantly familiar. It will come to me—I believe I am on the verge of putting the pieces of the puzzle into place.

* * *

Friday, April 4: I had the same dream last night. The sky was slightly lighter, more dusk than night, but the terrain was just as rugged, and the faces of the pedestrians partially hidden by a veil or a hood, but because there was more light it was easier to identify what could be seen of their expressions. There were two who resembled one another, not because they looked alike but because the expressions on their faces were similar, lips turned down, eyes still and startled, skin becoming more pale—it was as if there was a strip of material across the middle of their faces, accenting their irises and mouths, causing eyes to appear more bulging and lips more strained.

Work was better today—Fridays usually are, people are more upbeat, looking forward to the weekend. Craig will be back next Friday, but this weekend will be endless for me. I have no plans. My conversations with Craig have been erratic. He calls me at 9 PM Eastern time every evening, 8 PM Chicago time. He doesn't speak in any detail about his family over the phone. We are both distant and familiar with each other.

I decide to go into New York tomorrow, Saturday, maybe to the museum or to a play if I can get cheap tickets, or to an off-Broadway production. I get into bed early and pick up a book I found at my mother's house. She said her sister had given it to her to read, but she isn't interested in detective novels. My mother has always preferred more literary work. I like both—though tonight I am more inclined to read le Carré. I plump the pillows behind me, touch my scar as I always do each night, just to remember it is there. I take the book from the table next to the bed, open it up, and out falls an envelope with a card inside. More intrigued by the book than a card, I reach down and slide the envelope into my pocketbook, below me, on the rug next to the bed.

* * *

Morning, Saturday, April 5: Riding the train into Manhattan, I hold my pocketbook close to my chest; it is crowded and the strap could easily slip off my shoulder. I am thinking that I will see Craig in six more days, and then I begin to plan what I will do in the city today. There is an exhibit at the Met that I'd like to see. While Craig has been in Chicago, I have not called friends to get together—maybe I would have done so if he were away longer. Then my work week crosses my mind and I shut it out—I do not want to think about it until I tell Craig I believe I am less respected because he is not around. I have not mentioned it to him on the phone. When I spoke to him last night, he seemed far away, immersed in his Chicago family life.

My thoughts revolve around the exhibit I am about to see, how I have not contacted my friends, my work this past week, and my conversation with Craig last night—I switch from one to the next again and again. I regret I did not bring the le Carré book I started reading last night. With one hand I clutch my purse closer and look down. I notice the envelope I slipped into the outside pocket, and gingerly take it out. With one hand I carefully extract the card from the envelope. The image on the front of the card is of a Van Gogh painting, I believe. It is dated five years ago. The short note reads:

Dear Laura,

I haven't heard from you in a while. Just checking in to see if you are doing well. This pandemic, the isolation is awful. I need to see my new psychiatrist online—not very good in my opinion. I always enjoyed our conversations together, and feel at times I spoke too much about my life, and did not learn enough about yours. Though I do not understand your lifestyle, I hope you are content.

On another note, is Dr. Forester still practicing in Harrington? You know how challenging I found my sessions with him.

Should I bring this note to Dr. Forester? Not only because it is from a former patient of his, but because of my aunt, how she had invented the story of my scar. I'd like to ask him why she would have done so—was she aware that she had?

I clearly recall how I got the scar. I was seven or eight. I was in our basement with a friend. We were jumping on an old mattress. My parents had left it there, hoping to discard it. I jumped up and fell face-down on a wire that had poked through the mattress.

"Oh, I don't know, Stephen," she says, her eyes eluding his gaze. She feels his hand over hers and looks down.

It is dusk in the desert. They are sitting at a café close to their hotel. She smiles and says, "It is beautiful here." She takes a deep breath, then says, "Buying a vacation home out here at some point? I don't know."

"You've always been more conservative about money than me. But sometimes I think you need to go for what you want, dream a little."

"What about Nate?" she asks.

He shrugs. "We need to stop hovering over Nate. He needs to be free of us. We are constraining him."

"And *this* is why you want to have a vacation home across the country?"

Stephen smiles and says, "Let's go for a swim."

"After dinner?"

They wait until 10 PM to go to the pool. It is a hot night, and there are no other people at the swimming area. Stephen is restless. The California desert is her place, Brea discerns. The cacti, the exquisite Santa Rosa mountains, the intensity of the heat, the deep blue sky during the day, the subdued tones at dusk and the steep darkness at night.

A circle of small bulbs surrounds the broad, snake-shaped pool. A momentary silence. Stephen and Brea are alone. They sit in chaise lounges, and slowly begin to discuss their trip so far and where they will go next. Tonight is their last one in the desert.

Brea leans forward, unhooks the top part of her bathing suit. Standing, she moves swiftly forward and jumps into the pool. Stephen soon follows. The water caresses her body. She has never before felt more whole, more content. She looks over at Stephen, swimming laps; his strokes, how graceful they are, her eyes mist. She understands that she has contained him to a degree—her personality, too dramatic, at times, her spurious desires; their lack of authenticity prevented her from growing. She has gone past all the artifice, she hopes. Hasn't she? Isn't it the reason Stephen is more free?

A light drizzle, the air feels more raw since she left Penn Station, three hours ago. Lainie shivers, then walks more quickly. She went to the museum to see the exhibit on artists from the southwest, but it was surprisingly crowded. She will need to go again.

Walking the 30 blocks to Dr. Forester's apartment, she is slightly elated. She is surprised at how much she is looking forward to seeing him and Brea again, and at the same time unburdening herself of the card, asking his opinion of her aunt. It crosses her mind that she enjoys visiting Stephen and Brea. She recalls her parents, her father, and is filled with a deep sense of loss. How sudden her father's death had been—she had never really known him. Riding the elevator to the Foresters' apartment on the tenth floor, she asks herself, at twelve or thirteen how much did I understand of the adult world?

* * *

"My parents are not here—they are away," he says without inviting her in. "They are traveling, and won't be back for another week, at least."

Lainie turns away and says she will come at another time.

As she walks down the hallway, approaching the elevator in that even and forward-moving way, Nate studies her, the slope of her narrow shoulders. Then he moves quickly toward her; catching up, he asks if she'd like to come in for a moment. He needs to ask her something. She nods and follows him into the apartment.

When she sits down, she hands him a card, saying that she thinks his father might be interested and if he isn't—he can either destroy the note or return it to her. Then she jots down her address on a blank slip of paper she has taken from her pocketbook.

He finds her presence baffling, a curiosity. She adds that she doesn't believe the card will be of importance to her aunt anymore—her life has gone in an unexpected direction. She doesn't know if seeing this note from the past will be of use to her; as innocuous as it is, it could be disorienting to her.

Nate takes the card and slip of paper from her. "I remember you from Harrington."

"Is this what you wanted to say to me?"

"No. Why do you come to see my parents? Your fascination with them is unusual—why is it?"

Lainie shrugs, looks into his eyes, his puzzled expression, and imagines him on his scooter fourteen years ago, seeming innocent, tentative, but she sees he no longer is, that there is a subtle streak of anger about him that was not there in the past. She feels disappointed. "Private matters that I believed were over and have cropped up again or maybe not—it has to do with my aunt, who I lived with for a short while in Harrington—your father may or may not be interested." She pauses. "There is something else I'd like to talk to him about, but again he may not be interested. Let him know. You have my address—I will leave it up to him."

"Knowing my father, he will say it is up to you."

Lainie nods. She feels a growing frustration—what is holding her to these people? She doesn't know them. But she has returned. Then she hears Nate's voice.

"Do you remember me?" he asks, his voice abrupt. He doesn't know her or if what she is saying is true, but it no longer matters to him. He understands it has been an effort for her to come to his parents. It is evident in how she speaks of them—he supposes she believes it has been her duty to do so. He notices how she assesses him now.

"I lived with my aunt in Harrington for a year and a half, not very long," she says, her voice pensive.

"Then you would remember that time more easily, since it was for a short period—you would have recalled certain things about it. So either you remember me or you don't. It is simple, isn't it?" He smiles easily as he doesn't want her to feel pressured. He needs to know the truth. But he hears an edge, an insistence in his voice that she may find off-putting. It is important to him whether or not she remembers him. He only remembers a girl with a scar but doesn't know how old he was when he saw her, what year it was.

Her sigh is deep. "Yes, I remember you, but would not have recognized you now if I had not known you were Brea and Stephen's son. You have changed," she says assertively, then her voice lowers, "but don't we all, some in appearance, some in personality, others in both."

"What is it about me you would not have recognized?"

Ignoring his question, she says, "I remember you riding on your scooter, mostly alone. You seemed as sad and as isolated as I was. Even though I was accepted because people felt sorry for me because my father had died. But if I had stayed in Harrington longer, I do not know if I would have been as accepted—I think I would have fallen out with the people I was friendly with."

"I did not realize your father had died."

"We were not in the same class—I was a year ahead of you—that is why you did not know. My friends were protective, did not let the information get out beyond our group. His heart failed—it was unexpected, sudden. I never saw him ill, and I appreciated that, but it was devastating—my entire family changed once he died."

"And so you ended up in Harrington, living with your aunt?"

"Yes, exactly—people were good to me, friendly, though I felt alone most of the time, even when my friends believed I was content. I'd see you on your scooter and think, we are the same, lonely."

"I was alone after my closest friend left but I had never felt comfortable in Harrington. My parents did not have many friends. There were not happy there. I knew of no other place except New York—we'd visit my grandmother in the city. And so I knew there was another way of living, a place where we belonged. I was born there. But I was young and didn't think about it too much."

Lainie feels discouraged and says, "And the three of you have returned here."

He catches her gaze and says, "Stay a little longer. Are you meeting someone?"

"No, I'm free tonight. My partner is out of town."

"So is mine."

They casually laugh; it is beside the point.

Nate gets up and takes two glasses from the kitchen and then pours out some wine. He places the bottle on the coffee table, sits back on the couch. They drink in silence for a while.

"Did you really think we were both lonely in Harrington? Or, is it how you remember—is it easier to recall it in this way? Do you believe we are lonely now?" he asks, breaking the silence.

She speaks quietly, "I don't know. I am sure I thought that about you at the time, and now I don't think that at all. I don't believe either of us is lonely now." He sees how relaxed she tries to appear. She is tired, he thinks.

"Your scar—how did you get it? I remember noticing it, but then I forgot about it; it is not very apparent, and in a way it is attractive."

"A childhood accident—jumping on an old mattress, I fell face-down on a wire poking through."

"It must have been painful." He leans forward in his seat.

Lainie shrugs. She cannot remember. "We did not see each other many times, only a handful maybe?"

"What may have been the last time I noticed you is what I remember most. You did not see me, I think. You were with someone, a boy, and you were holding hands—I saw you both go inside a garage and I waited for you to come out but you didn't right away, and then you did. It was about an hour later. I waited behind a tree. I was curious yet understood what was happening—it was the first time I ever had. I mean about someone my age. You see, I was accustomed to adults being this way. I was young and would notice my grandmother flirting with other men, and then my mother too, sometimes it was because she was acting in a play, and once it was real life, but I imagine for her it was acting in real life too. I had forgotten about you until I saw you leave this apartment last September. And my parents then told me you had come to see them. The memory suddenly came back."

"Memories are like that, sometimes they never leave and at other times they disappear and suddenly return. Though I never have much confidence in a memory, sometimes it could be accurate, and at other times it might not be. Hope I did not disillusion you. I have no recollection of what you are saying, but I believe you. You seem twelve or thirteen again. Not often do you find someone of our age who has retained a degree of innocence. I think our generation is jaded without realizing we are so. We fully believe we are idealistic."

Nate shrugs and pours each of them more wine.

"What do you do?" she asks.

"If you want to know what I want to be, I am not sure. Now I teach children who are hospitalized how to draw."

She nods.

He crosses his ankles and takes a sip of wine, thinking how succinct and analytical she is.

Lainie glances out the window and sees it is dark. The lights in the apartment appear dimmer. Exhausted—she does not have the energy to take the train home to Connecticut. She looks at Nate, sinking into the couch, his legs resting on the coffee table, his face is in shadow. His thoughts are on something else now, she realizes. She has been vaguely aware that a classical radio station has been playing. She has never had a strong knowledge of classical music, but she recognizes the piece—Beethoven's Moonlight Sonata. She looks past Nate and out the window, searching for the moon—it is not visible to her. She gets up, goes over to the couch and slumps down next to him, rests her feet on the coffee table, checks her watch. Craig will be calling soon.

V

Lainie, about to leave the apartment, grasps the doorknob; then, dropping her hand, she turns to Nate. It is 7 AM. He notices how the early morning sun lights up her scar. He thinks of a flame. He reaches out, touching it. She steps back. His hand still on her face, he says, "You do not need to have it—it can be taken care of, I believe." But as these words escape him, he knows she will never have it removed—it is part of who she is as much as her sense of purpose, her detachment. It protects her.

She meets his gaze, There is disappointment in her eyes. She lifts her hand. A slight wave. And he understands she will not come again to his parents, or to him.

Closing the door, he barely hears her walking toward the elevator. He thinks of how she was at thirteen or fourteen, the same thoughtful way of raising her brows, studying him from across the road. His response had been to hold more tightly on to the handlebars of his scooter. He hadn't thought her feelings were similar to his. He had been unaware of her father's death; though now he believes most of the people in Harrington had known of it.

That memory had come to him, easily, unexpectedly, out of context. It had been last fall, a month after he'd seen her leave his parents' apartment. He was with Adrianna, crossing a street. They were on their way to see an off-Broadway play, *Pygmalion.*

His mother had highly recommended this production of Shaw's play. And as he walked a few steps behind Adrianna, the memory flashed across his mind in a real and visceral way. Why now, he wondered, was he recalling her emerging from the garage, holding on to a boy's hand, the detachment in her eyes.

What he had focused on at the time had been her scar. His imagination had been wild; he had wondered if she was a witch or an evil person—he just hadn't known and so he purposely had refused to allow thoughts of her to enter his mind. He had been filled with anger—he had not known why he was feeling this throbbing sensation within—he had wanted to fight back like a child whose favorite toy had been taken from him. There had been a hard sensuality in her dispassion that had awakened something within him, frightening him, attracting him.

Eventually his strong feelings dissipated. He became resolved, had disciplined himself not to think of her. As days and months passed, he had come across her less and less and so she had become less of a presence to him and then he saw her no more. He had gone to boarding school in Boston and had not come upon her again until he had passed her in the hallway last September. But even then he hadn't been certain, had at first only experienced a mild sense of familiarity. It was because of how she walked in an even and forward-moving way. A distinctive step and the same faraway look in her eyes, and then, there was her scar.

Adrianna returns from her trip before his parents do. Sitting across from Nate in their favorite restaurant, in a room with deep pink wallpaper, a violinist playing close by, she tells him she has fallen in love with an Italian in Venice. "Nate, the problem has been that though I like you very much, respect you, even admire you, I am not certain I have ever been in love with you." Her voice is insistent, her dark eyes not meeting his. She pauses, then says, "And we met when the world was a different place."

"No, Adrianna, we met before then, at the bottom of the Spanish Steps," he says affirmatively.

"It doesn't count, Nate."

He looks across the table at her, feeling uneasy at first, then a stab of pain. "I do not know what you mean—of course it matters," he answers, hearing how resolute he sounds. He imagines her in Venice sitting at a café in the Piazza San Marco, her top lip raised, searching. He doesn't ask if she has fallen in love from a distance—in her imagination—or in reality.

They leave the restaurant, part, and believe they might not see each other again. But maybe they will, he thinks, hoping her infatuation is short-lived and that again she will return to him. Though he is not certain. Maybe her passion for this mysterious Italian is more real than he believes. Or, maybe she hasn't actually spoken to him? An illusion?

Over the next few days, Nate stays in his parents' apartment, often thinking of his grandfather and father, their lives.

The afternoon before his mother and father return, he attempts to figure out what he should do next. Not plans, but a mosaic of images comes to mind: Adrianna at the bottom of the Spanish Steps, her concerned expression; Lainie walking out of the garage, holding hands with the boy; how sunlight flooded her scar the morning she left his parents' apartment, her slight wave; his mother touching his shoulder, telling him to wait outside his father's office; his mother's director, his hands on her face, her waist during rehearsals, touching her hair as he knelt close to her; his father intently reading a history book, his shoulders forward. Nate was deeply moved at those times, as he is now.

He thinks of himself at twelve, sitting in the waiting area outside his father's office that early June day, how he had anticipated the summer ahead. He'd been bothered by the Van Gogh painting hanging on the wall. Instead he thought of the copy of the Homer in his father's home office—two boys sitting in a pasture. He recalls how his father had said of the painting that he believed there was much stirring within those two boys—their fears and longings were just beginning to evolve. How their lives unfold, he had added later while hanging up the painting, Nate leaning close to him, would depend on such moments of reflection.

Nate stands, looks across the apartment, his gaze catches a shaft of light falling across the Matisse art book on the coffee table, extending to the door of his parents' bedroom, partially open. He steps closer to it and inhales the conflicting scent of his mother's perfume. Then he goes to the threshold of his father's small office, spots the replica of the Winslow Homer painting on the wall. It appears different than it did in the spacious home office in Harrington, less compelling, more defined, distant. He turns away, moves toward the foyer, and opens the door.

With long strides, the cold April wind in his face, he walks at a quick pace, as if freeing himself from something or someone—Lainie's scar? Her dispassion? The ghost of his father's father? His parents' puzzling marriage?

Three blocks to go. The sun is strong. He believes he sees her standing in front of his apartment building. Uncertain, he pauses. Maybe not. A deep longing. He takes another stride, hoping it is Adrianna.

www.ingramcontent.com/pod-product-compliance
Lightning Source LLC
LaVergne TN
LVHW091001080826
845145LV00003B/1077